Warning

This book contains sexually explicit scenes and adult language and may be considered offensive to some readers. This book is intended for adults ONLY. Please store your books wisely, where they cannot be accessed by under-aged readers.

Dear Miss Ricci

You don't know this yet, but you will be my wife.

Sincerely
Your soon-to-be husband

He thought I was his—that's what his emails indicated.
He thought that because our families signed on the dotted line many years ago, it was a done deal.
But I ran away from that life for a reason.
Little did I know, he would find me. And he wasn't going to take no for an answer.
Crue wanted me to be his wife.
And all I wanted was him in my bed.

CHAPTER 1
Rya

F ourteen years ago

MY FEET DRAG on the cobblestones. It's hot, and I don't mean cool-breeze-flowing-up-my-shirt hot. I mean, damn *hot*. It's meant to start cooling down in Rome in September, but here we are, and I wish I could tear off my clothes. But my father may very well kill me if I did that, even if he isn't here right now.

I know he would find out.

That's what happens when he has connections —everywhere.

I walk past restaurants, and people nod to me and quickly look away.

I'm only sixteen, but they all know who I am. It's in their best interests, and they would be silly not to. My sister laughs as she kicks off her shoes and starts running ahead, not concerned about our father's wrath or how we're viewed or should be acting. She's three years younger than me and somewhat free-spirited. I have no doubt she'll be giving Papa a run for his money when she turns sixteen.

I look back to Marco, who has basically been our bodyguard for as long as I can remember. He's shaking his head but trying to hide a smirk. She wants to see the Colosseum together one more time before I leave. Butterflies dance in my stomach with excited energy at the thought of the one-way ticket to New York I'll be putting to use in only a few hours. Who am I to deny my little sister one more outing before I leave? It also gives me time to say goodbye for the last time to my friends.

"Rya." Tourists walk around us as Honey yells out my name. She's easy to spot even amidst the crowd with her bright pink dress and dangling shoes in hand. We are a stark contrast as I wear my sandals with baggy jeans and a cropped T-shirt. I sure as hell should have worn a dress, it would have been much cooler.

"I don't want you to go." Honey runs at me, her arms wrap around my waist, and I awkwardly brush my hand down her back to return the hug. Honey's hair is long and chestnut colored—she takes after her mother, my stepmother—whereas mine is almost caramel in color.

I'm going to live with my mother, which does not make my father happy. But I feel like living here, I can't really *live*.

I know that's not the entire reason.

What I mean is I can't live without being watched.

And I'm always watched living here.

I hate it.

I want to sneak out.

I want to kiss a boy I don't know.

I want to be felt up without the fear of one of my father's men shooting him for touching me.

I want it all.

I want my freedom.

And yet, it breaks my heart to leave Honey. I love her. Yes, she can be annoying like any other little sister. But for as long as I can remember, I have put her to sleep every night by reading a book to her.

Who's going to read to her now?

Her mother drinks—a lot.

Our father—he's always busy.

So it's just her and me against the world.

It's been fun.

But I want to escape.

No, I need to escape so badly that I want to pull my own hair from my scalp. But how do I explain that to a thirteen-year-old?

"I'm sure you and Papa will come visit me in New York, and I'll come back here for visits as well," I say, trying to reassure her.

She's tall, almost my height now.

Her mother was a supermodel whom Papa met at Fashion Week in Milan. She saw his power and money, and that was more than enough of an attraction to stay. She gave him a child, hoping it would be a boy, but out came Honey instead. Beautiful Honey. The only way you can tell we're sisters is our eyes—almost cat-like in shape and silverish in color.

Marco stays back as we weave through the last of the crowd. I spot Angel straight away. She waves at me, but what stops me in my tracks are the two men behind her. They look older, not our age, at least I think. But possibly not quite as old as the men who surround my father and stare at me in ways that make me extremely uncomfortable.

"Rya, hurry up. I have a drink for you," she shouts through the crowd, not caring what they might think. I look over my shoulder at Marco, who shakes his head but doesn't say anything to stop me.

I pull back from Honey and look down. "Go and stay with Marco. I won't be long. I have to say goodbye."

She obediently nods as she looks over my shoulder, curious about the men.

"Go," I encourage again, with a huff of a laugh she walks away. Most definitely, her curiosity is going to give Papa grief.

I make my way over to meet Angel. She smells of fresh linen. I've always loved that scent, as it almost feels homey. Our laundry has never had a scent. It's as though it conspires with my stepmother to ensure nothing about our house is homey.

Angel's arms tightly embrace me as she utters, "I'll miss you when you're in New York." I struggle in her tight hold, trying to take in a deep breath. I'm going to miss her too. But this is way too many hugs for my liking in one day.

"New York?" someone says from behind her.

She pulls back but holds my arms. I look over her shoulder at the two men, both good-looking. But one —the one who's looking at me as if he's almost angry —holds my stare.

"This is Crue and his brother Dominic." She waves at them. "Friends of the family," she says with an eye roll. "Ignore them. They saw me sneak out of Mother's party and insisted they come, or they were going to tell her I snuck this." She pulls out a bottle of wine with a Cheshire cat smile. "And this," she says, gesturing to a small bottle of whiskey shoved between her breasts. She pulls me in for another hug.

As she does, she passes me the bottle, and I glance over my shoulder to ensure Marco isn't watching before I lift the small bottle and drain half the whiskey. Dominic whistles before he steps forward and places his arm around Angel. I embrace the burn down my throat, but I am confused. She hadn't told me about a new man.

Angel happily takes the bottle and shrugs him off, saying, "Dominic, knock it off," before taking a swig.

"I recall you calling me God the other night."

I gasp at his words.

Angel's cheeks blush and she hands me the bottle of wine, leaning in close as if that's the chaser.

"Don't judge. I was sad about you leaving. He was there."

"You lost your virginity to him?" I ask while opening the bottle of wine, and then I take a sip.

"Yep," he answers, obviously overhearing us.

"Rya." I turn around to see Marco has Honey leaning against him. She's tired. I swear, sometimes she still reminds me of a child.

"I'm not ready to go yet," I tell him.

"Your father—" he starts, but I cut him off.

"Will do nothing. I'll be back later."

Marco shoots a glare at the bottle still in my hand. "I'll come back for you. That's all I am giving," he says.

I nod and give him my sickly-sweet smile. One that he doesn't seem all too delighted by, but that always works for Honey. Marco is basically our uncle, not by blood but by marriage. We love him, but he always listens to orders from Papa. There are times when he offers me a sliver of freedom, but it's not often.

I watch them walk off and feel someone step up next to me.

"You a princess or something?" I don't even turn to him. Earlier, he stared at me as if I had a second head. Or like he was mad at me. Instead, I shake my head and focus on Marco and Honey as they disappear into the crowd.

"That's the princess leaving," I say, lifting the bottle to my lips and drinking as much as I can.

"Whoa, there. Just because you aren't a princess doesn't mean you should trust us," he says.

I pull the bottle from my lips.

"Trust us?" I ask, now finally turning to look at him. His skin is tanned, his black shirt clings to his body—possibly from the heat—and his brows scrunch together as he stands there and lets me simply stare. Crue says nothing, just licks his lips. I seem to do the same thing, watching his dark eyes drop to mine. There is a silent intensity in that stare. And if I didn't know any better, I would say his breathing got heavier.

"How old are you?" Crue asks.

"Sixteen," I reply. He shakes his head and steps back. "Why?" Crue looks over his shoulder at Angel and Dominic, who are making out, him holding her up and her legs wrapped around his waist.

Right, I'm on my own with this one, then.

"Are you leaving?" he asks.

I don't know why, but every hair on my body raises. It feels like there is an underlying question, but I answer anyway, "Yes."

"Why?" Crue takes the bottle of wine from me, lifts it to his lips, and takes a sip. He offers it back to me, and when he does, our fingers touch.

Butterflies take flight in my stomach. What the fuck! So I pull the bottle away and take a sip, hoping to drown them out.

I don't think I'll ever see this man again, so there's no point in feeling any sexual tension around him.

"I'm going to live with my mother. How old are you?" I ask, and Crue smirks.

"Nineteen." He looks at his brother when Angel

shouts Dominic's name and slaps him. They're still giggling and making out.

"How old is your brother?" My eyes don't follow his. Instead, they trace the outline of his jaw, the slight stubble of hair growing there, and I wonder if it's as sharp as it looks.

"Almost eighteen." Okay, he isn't too much older than Angel. Crue looks back at me. "What do you plan to do in New York?"

"I plan to not have my father arrange my marriage. It's why I'm leaving," I answer, averting my gaze. He can't force me to marry anyone if I'm not here. It's basically selling ownership of my freedom, and I am not down for that.

"Hmm," is his only response.

"What about you? Are you destined to marry anyone?" I ask sarcastically.

"If I choose."

"Lucky you," I grumble.

"I wouldn't say that." Crue smirks.

"Why?" I ask, becoming invested in this conversation.

"Because the one I'm arranged to marry is running off to New York."

The bottle of wine in my hand feels red hot and I want to drop it to relieve the burn.

Did he just say what I think he did?

No.

"Bit stunned?" Crue asks. "Figured I would come meet the one I am matched to." He turns and walks off, while I stand there, confused and slowly shaking my head.

I was told I had a match, and because of that, I had worked out a plan to get away.

Escape.

To be free.

Crue is to be my husband when I turn eighteen.

THIS MAN who is walking away from me right now.

"Stop!" I call after him.

He does, and when he looks back, I rethink my decision to leave. Should I stay? How bad would it be to be married to someone like him?

I'm not really sure.

"Why would you want to know?" I ask.

His hands slide into the pockets of his dark jeans, and I walk closer to stand by his side.

"If you had a choice, would you marry?" I question.

His response is quick and unyielding. "Yes. My father did it, and his father before that."

That means Crue is next in line.

And his family?

I've heard horror stories about his family.

My father is powerful, but his family... well, they don't play around. And it seems that I'm about to break a family tradition. Marriage to a Monti. It's why my father was hoping for a boy. His generation skipped being married to a Monti, but I guess now that's not the case.

"Do you not want to be in love? Not forced to marry someone not of your choosing?" I ask, baffled at his answer to my previous question.

"You may be able to run away, but I cannot." His gaze slides to his brother before coming back to me. "If I'm not married by thirty-four, I will come find you, princess."

His words take me aback.

"What if I am married?"

"That will be bad for your husband." He smirks, then strides off.

CHAPTER 2

Rya

Today

Dear Miss Ricci

You don't know this yet, but you will be my wife.

Sincerely
Your soon-to-be husband

"THIRTY. OH MY GOD, RYA, THIRTY." Monica throws her arms around my neck. My dress is half zipped up, and I struggle to get it all the way up because of her. I blow out a half-frustrated huff that's assumed to be because I am struggling with the dress. But my mind keeps drawing back to the email I received earlier. It came from an email address I don't recognize, and I put it straight in the trash when I saw it. Tonight isn't the night to worry over random emails, and it's probably a scam or something anyway.

"I know. Now, please pull away so I can get dressed." I huff and tap her naked back. Monica couldn't care less though—nudity to her is like clothes. The number of times I have gone over to her house and she has been butt-ass naked is insane. At least this time, I suppose she's wearing a bra and panties. She also knows I hate affection, but she always needs it.

"I'm just excited, and you look so beautiful." Monica finally pulls back and claps her hands. I zip up my teal dress, and I have the impression her excitement is more over the dress than me. Her breasts bounce, barely strapped in by her silky bronze bra, as she lets out another shrill noise. She intends to wear a low-cut dress that suits her figure perfectly, meaning she can, if she wants, have any man she desires. I've watched it happen multiple times throughout our friendship.

My dress, however, is slightly different. The teal color—different from the black I usually wear for every occasion, from work to social gatherings to dates—complements my sun-kissed skin and eye color, which is as close to silver as anyone could get. It's only because the sales assistant at Macy's begged me to try on this dress that I fell in love with it in the first place. So here I am, stepping out of my comfort zone and wearing something different. I guess turning thirty is a new decade and all.

"Thanks, though maybe I should be wearing black. You know, for the end of my twenties," I tell her. "Like those photoshoots they do where it's like a death."

"Please, those bitches don't realize your thirties are amazing. You stop giving a fuck so much more than in your twenties." She reaches for her red dress and slips it on, throwing her bra to the wind. "Is any of your family coming?"

"No. Though, an old friend is going to be visiting. I haven't seen her since I was sixteen." I smile. After all these years, I'm excited to see Angel, but I can't help a sliver of guilt for not returning home for over fourteen years. "I'll go back eventually and visit them. It's just that once I'd finished college and started working, I haven't stopped," I tell her, but she already knows the facts.

"And they can always visit you," she replies, turning around expectantly for me to zip up her dress.

"Now, let's walk out into that room that's already filled with people who love you and let loose. You promised me tonight you'll get freaky." She says 'freaky' with a little side shuffle in what I think is supposed to be a dance.

And I know there'll be no getting out of it. I came straight from the office and quickly changed in the back room of the hotel where my birthday party is starting. And I know Monica will be dragging me to God knows what clubs.

I slip on my black heels and give myself a once-over in the small mirror. I don't know if I was meant to look any different at thirty, but I look fucking hot. I can't remember the last time I had a night out, but tonight feels like *the night*. I might even pick up a man. It's been a while, and I certainly have an itch to scratch.

I follow Monica through the door, and shouts immediately erupt when people start to sing "Happy Birthday." I recognize most people straight away from work. I awkwardly receive hugs and kisses on the cheek as I walk through the crowded room. Monica's already ahead of me, beelining for the bottles of champagne and giving me that much-needed elixir so I feel less awkward under this type of spotlight. I've never been much for celebrating birthdays, but you know, thirty and all, so I don't have a lot of choice.

I begin a light discussion with one of my colleagues on our recent case.

"I just don't know how you do it," one of the interns says, absolutely baffled.

"It's because she's one of the best," my boss says, intruding on our conversation. I've been working for him since graduating college.

I take a small sip of my champagne. "The stats from the last four years would clarify I *am* the best at our firm."

"A lawyer?" someone asks from behind me. I hear the heavy accent before I turn around, and I'm stunned when I see the speaker. My feet don't want to move, and the white noise around me disappears.

He's here.

My heart skips a beat.

Holy shit, he's actually here.

I didn't think Crue would hold to his words from so long ago. In truth, I had completely forgotten about it until right now. Surely, he's not here for that. But here he stands, looking better than ever. The once clean-skinned man now has ink peeking out from his black collar and up his neck, with such confidence it makes you want to look away. But I've been dealing with powerful men all my life, and I've become unyielding even to someone like him.

Is he here for *that* reason?

Why else would he be here?

I'm so confused, yet with an audience around us, I'm quick to dismiss any further attention. But, damn, it's hard when Crue looks like *that*. Almost every woman is looking in our direction now.

"Crue," I say, smiling. His dark eyes fall to my lips at the sound of his name coming from them.

"Princess," he replies, but it's flat as if he's forced to be here.

Which confuses me even more.

"I don't know what to say," I tell him, pushing a strand of hair behind my ear while the other hand clutches my glass a little too hard.

"Happy birthday," he says. "I don't exactly do apologies, so I'm not going to bother with what I'm about to do."

My fake smile falters.

About to do? What does he mean?

And then I understand when he reaches into his jacket, and I see the glint of the gun before he even grasps it.

It all happens in slow motion.

I'm unsure what to do, but my body seems frozen.

I moved away from Italy all those years ago to remove myself from the violence that surrounded me.

And yet, after all these years, here it is. Standing in front of me.

Is he about to kill me?

Except his eyes are no longer on me, and his hand is now on his gun. There aren't more than twenty people mingling in the back room of the restaurant connected to the hotel. I stare in horror as he pulls the gun from a holster. And before I can ask any questions, he shoots.

I flinch at the sound, and his gaze darts back to me. Someone screams—a lot of people do, actually—and he slides the gun back into the holster, that foreboding gaze impenetrable. And then he smirks—actually fucking smirks—with no care in the world for what he has done.

"I'll be seeing you *real* soon, princess." He turns and casually walks out, two men flanking him. My legs are shaking, and my heart is hammering, though I'd never let him see that. I wait until he's gone before I dare look elsewhere, like being on high alert and watching a predator leave the vicinity.

What is Crue doing here in New York?

And who the fuck did he just shoot?

"Rya! Rya!" Monica grabs my arm with shaking hands. "We have to move. We have to go."

He's not coming back, though. Crue's done what

he needed to do, and now he's gone. Before I can think better of it, I turn to my left, and that's when I see a pair of boots just visible around the bottom hem of a tablecloth, and a pool of blood staining the floor.

My boss.

Dead.

And the man who has filled so many of my dreams over the years was the one who killed him.

Fuck.

CHAPTER 3

Crue

"Are you sure that was the right decision?" Dominic asks.

I crack my neck from side to side as I look at him. "Are you second-guessing my decision?" I raise a brow at him.

"No, of course not." He twirls his wedding band around his finger. "But Angel wanted to see her."

"Angel can see her, just not tonight," I explain. Not that I fucking have to—he should know better—but Dominic loves to push my buttons.

"Do you plan to tell her that?" Dominic asks, looking over his shoulder to where Angel is throwing things around because she's incredibly mad that we told her she had to stay back while we worked.

"Nope, she isn't my wife." I reach for the bottle of

whiskey, and he shakes his head.

"Sometimes I hate you," Dominic whispers.

"Good. I'm not here to make friends," I remind him.

"I'm your fucking brother," he growls.

"And? I'm *not* our father. You should know that."

Dominic might have had a soft spot for our father, but if he knew why I'd really put a bullet in our father's head, then he might not second-guess me. Not that I give a shit. I worked and killed to get to where I am so I wouldn't have to answer to anyone. *Blood or not.*

"Well, maybe he isn't so much of a devil as we all thought. Because you sure as shit are worse."

"I take that as a compliment," I say, lifting the glass to my lips. Reaching for my phone, I type up an email, with her name in the header.

Dear Miss Ricci
It was a pleasure to see you again tonight.
I hope you will soon accept an invitation to join me for
dinner as an apology for ruining your birthday.
And please note, I never apologize.
At your earliest convenience.
Reply.
Crue

CHAPTER 4

Rya

I read the email, then re-read it again.

It can't be real, right? No way.

I shake my head as I look up at the police officer who has been asking me questions for hours on end. He says something and then hands me a card. My once beautiful teal dress is now covered in dirt. Sitting on the sidewalk in New York city is not for the faint-hearted.

"Are you okay?" I look up at the question. Monica's shoulders sag and the distant and empty stare tells me she is sad, which is very unlike her. But I suppose under the circumstances, it's expected.

"If I'd have worn black, do you think this still would have happened?" I ask, causing her to smirk.

"Okay, next time, stick to the black." She offers me

her hand and pulls me up. I wipe my hands down my dress once I am on my feet.

"They say it's a pretty open and shut case, or so I overheard them talking. Someone said they caught the guy, and nothing else will be happening." When she says the words, I look down at my phone. *Open and shut case, my ass.* But if you have influence in your name, you can get away with murder these days. *Especially* him.

Quickly typing and sending a message, I wait for my mailbox to tell me if it's true. I don't know whether he'll reply immediately or even at all.

Or if it's him to begin with.

Is this really you?

I DON'T KNOW what else to say, but when my phone dings and his name pops up in my emails, I know it's him.

Dear Miss Ricci
Should I come over now?

Reply.
Crue.

REPLY. Why does he sign off with that?

It's demanding.

And rude.

And Crue being here might be problematic.

So I ignore it, slide my phone back into my purse, and look at Monica. She doesn't know much about where I came from, and I don't intend to share it with her. She's met my mother a few times and knows my father lives in Italy. That's it. How do you tell someone that your father is a killer?

You don't.

"I'm going to go home. I'm not exactly in the mood to party anymore," I tell her.

She nods and walks with me. My apartment isn't too far, and thankfully, it has security, so I shouldn't have to worry about that psycho. My job pays well, and it's the first thing I invested in.

Well, I guess it did pay well until my boss died. Hopefully, that won't affect my work. I've been with this firm since straight out of college and worked my way up. I'm a good lawyer, and defending criminals came naturally to me. But I know despite our outstanding reputation, even this will make headlines. Sure, we've made a few enemies in the past, but I can't understand why Crue, of all people, would target my boss. But that feels like a Monday problem because I'm dead tired.

"I may catch a cab, but I'll walk you back first," Monica says.

"I can handle myself, and it's close. Go home, cuddle your cat." I step out to the road and wave down a cab. She seems torn about leaving me, so I open the door and nod for her to get in.

"How are you so relaxed?" she whispers. "I mean, he did it right next to you."

"I'm fine. I deal with criminals, remember. Go to bed." I reluctantly give her a one-armed hug before she climbs into the cab, and then I watch as she drives off. I take the short walk home to decompress.

When I arrive at my apartment, the doorman opens the door as I approach. He gives me a once-over, most likely because of the state of my dress, but says nothing. As I step into the elevator and press the button for my floor, my mind drifts with so many variables.

Crue. Why is he here, and why now?

My boss. What was Crue's objective?

But I try to push those thoughts away, knowing I'll become obsessed with it like my cases. And tonight, I want to sleep. I exit the elevator and unlock my door before I step in and shut it behind me.

"Your dress is dirty."

I don't think, I act.

Spinning, I shoot my hand out straight for the throat of whoever is behind me. He catches it though, and drops his head to the side. But that doesn't stop me. My knee comes up and meets with his junk. Crue bends over, his hand letting go of mine as I fist his hair and pull him all the way down. I sidestep him, intent on getting to the kitchen, but he reaches for me, grips the side of my dress while he's still bent over, and I kick again, only this time my heel meets his ribs. "Fucking hell," he shouts. And just as I start to move again, both of his arms circle my waist and pin my hands to my sides.

I'm breathing heavily, and so is he. I try to wiggle away, but he grunts and tightens his hold, keeping me in place.

"Could you not make my cock hard after you just fucking kneed it," he grumbles. I pause at his words, my body straightening and locking tight. "Who taught you to fight?" Crue asks.

"Let me go."

"*Who* taught you to fight?" he demands, and I have the distinct impression he isn't a man who often asks questions twice.

"My father put me in jujitsu when I was eight. When I moved here, his requirement was for me to continue any form of fighting. I chose kickboxing," I tell him, trying to get my hands free. "Now... Let. Me. Go."

"Lethal," he whispers near my ear before dropping his arms around my waist and stepping back.

I turn around to face him. "Why are you here?"

"Are you married?" Crue asks, looking down at my hand.

"No." My brows scrunch together in confusion.

"I'm thirty-three," he tells me.

"Oookay."

And it hits me.

All at once.

How could I forget?

Probably because I just watched him kill someone. Was this really what this was all about? The arranged marriage between our families?

"I'll pick you up at seven tomorrow. Do *not* be late. One thing I do not tolerate is lateness."

"Do not tolerate?" I ask. "What does that even mean?"

"The last man who was late to one of my meetings lost a finger," Crue explains as he heads to the door. Then he pulls it open and walks out without a backward glance.

I'm left standing there, wondering what the hell is happening and how he managed to get inside my apartment.

SOMETIMES I WISH time could be brought forward, and today is that day. I wish it was Monday because I spent all day wondering what I plan to do. I know this matter is above the police, and besides, I've dealt with my fair share of powerful men, especially the criminal type. And one thing I know is that they can be unrelenting. And in the way of a calling card, Crue put a bullet in my boss's head. So begrudgingly, I must go because who knows how else he might lash out. Maybe a dinner setting will allow us to speak about it in a civilized manner. At least, that's what I am trying to convince myself of. Crue emailed me the address and told me not to be late. *Again.*

I'm totally going to be late.

It's already thirty minutes past the time he wanted to meet, and I'm still in the car he sent to fetch me.

The driver has not commented about my tardiness, so either he doesn't know or doesn't care.

I intend to be late.

Crue can deal with it.

And what the hell do you wear to see a man who told you once a long time ago that he intends to marry you when he turns thirty-four? It's such a weird number. And, to be honest, after a few years, I forgot all about it, thinking he didn't really mean it.

That was until last night.

The car comes to a stop, and I look toward the double doors of the building. Maybe I should have the driver turn around and take me home.

Might be a smart idea.

But before I can even think of telling the driver to take off, my door is open, and I'm met with a smiling man.

"He's going to be so pissed you're late." He says it with a smirk.

I'm confused at first. *Who is this man?* And then I see the similarities to Crue. They both have soft, dark hair, but where Crue has a slight wave to his, Dominic's is stick straight. Where Dominic's skin is ink-free, Crue has tattoos.

"It's good to see you. Angel never shuts up about seeing you."

Dominic offers me his hand, and I take it and pull myself out. When I'm standing in front of him, I notice his wedding ring. Last I heard they were still an item. But did something change in that time?

"You see Angel?" I ask, remembering she was supposed to be on her way to visit me.

"She's my wife. Did she forget to tell you?"

What?

I offer a polite smile, the one I use when I'm in court. My silence, however, is enough of an answer. I knew her and Dominic Monti had been a thing since I left Italy. But over the years we didn't talk about it much. And I never asked if she'd changed partners. We didn't really go into depth about our lovers... or perhaps because I was the only who had multiple lovers. We mostly spoke about the stuff we binge-watch on television, what's happening at work, and changes with the families back at home. Small things—unimportant things.

But how could she not tell me she was married? And to Dominic Monti?

Dominic looks over his shoulder and into the restaurant. "You better go before he kills both of us."

I nod and clutch my bag to my stomach. My heels click on the sidewalk as I approach the double doors. I spot Crue at a table in the back as soon as they open.

His eyes are already on me, and his hands are fisted together on the table. The hostess leads me to him as a waitress places food on his table.

"Is there anything else?" the waitress asks as the hostess pulls out my seat opposite him.

"No, that will be all."

They give us polite smiles and then leave.

"You're late," he says, a tic running through his jaw.

I nonchalantly shrug. "Time moves differently in New York."

His jaw tics again, and he picks up a knife and cuts into his steak. "Eat," he orders.

I look at the food in front of me and grimace. "I'll be fine."

"Don't like steak?" he asks as he takes a bite. I watch as he chews slowly, his lips moving with each bite.

He looks like he's trying to contain his fury. I am not sure for how long and I take some pleasure in knowing that.

"No," I reply.

"We are at a steak house," he points out as he swallows and lifts his glass of wine to his lips.

"That was your choice," I remind him.

"And you were late," he adds, with a hint of anger

radiating from him.

Definitely the grudge-holding type.

"So?" I shrug.

"I warned you not to be late."

"And I couldn't care less what you warned," I fire back.

He sucks a hiss through his teeth before he goes back to cutting his steak. "Who told you it was okay to have *this much* attitude?" he asks, and a rattled laugh escapes me.

"Is this a joke?" I reply, leaning in.

"You have forgotten where you came from and what women mean to men."

"And what precisely do they mean?" I lean back in my chair, crossing my arms over my chest.

"That they obey and do what men say."

I blow out a frustrated breath. Then I laugh, shaking my head, disbelieving in how *that world* followed me all the way to New York.

No, *he* has followed me all the way here.

"Is this why I'm here, for you to tell me how I should act?" I ask, leaning in again and tilting my head.

"Are you not afraid of me?" he questions, leaning in until only a breath separates us.

"No."

"You should be." He smirks.

CHAPTER 5

Crue

This woman.

Who the fuck is she?

Rya is nothing like the stories I've been told. She is feisty, independent, and everything I shouldn't want.

Everything I *don't* want.

I'm supposed to marry a woman who will blend in, who will have no qualms staying in the background and doing as she's told.

So why do I feel Rya wouldn't be any of those things?

She sits across from me in her little black dress, legs long and tanned, and her hair, which reminds me of caramel, is half up and half down.

I fucking hate caramel.

Those eyes, though.

The fuck-me eyes that look at you with so much fucking sex, it oozes from her.

It's a strange contrast.

The silver of her eyes to the caramel of her hair.

You would think they wouldn't match.

But they do.

Fuck, they match perfectly.

"Is this all I'm here for?" She waves her hand at the food, leaning back and drawing away the temptation. Barely. "Because I need to eat, and this..." she looks down at her plate "... I will *not* eat."

"What do you want to eat?" I ask. "Fucking salad?"

"Anything that doesn't have meat. Or that comes from an animal."

I lift my hand, and the waitress quickly returns to the table.

"Tell her what you want."

She checks around at other tables and spots a plate of seasoned vegetables.

"Can I please have one of those?"

The waitress nods and quickly scurries away.

"Really?" I ask, raising a brow.

"Do you have an issue with my choice of food?" Rya asks.

Palpable silence fills the space. She's not in any way

unnerved by me, and I find that as much irritating as I do fascinating.

"Why am I here, Crue?" she asks, unimpressed. How my name rolls off her tongue draws my gaze to her lips again. Those filthy, fuckable lips. I grab my glass of whisky and down the contents. She should not be *this* fucking tempting. But defiant girls do have to be shown a lesson and broken in—it's how it has always been.

"I plan to marry you," I state.

She pales, and her crossed arms drop. "No," she replies.

"No?"

"That's what I said. I am guessing you don't hear that word too often?" she says, some color coming back to her face.

"Do you think your father would agree with you saying no to me?"

"He doesn't have a say. I left. Therefore, he has no say."

"Just because you left does not mean he doesn't have control of you."

"That's precisely what it means."

"You know it was him who paid for your education?"

"Of course I do."

"And you know he's had you watched for all these years, right?"

"Watched?" She shakes her head. "No, he hasn't."

"Of course he has." I grin. "Monica's the perfect friend, right?" I say, dropping the bomb right on her.

Rya laughs at that, but I know she's a clever girl.

"That's not true. Monica would epically suck at being a spy."

"She's not a spy, but she is paid highly to hang out with you. Be your friend." I study her as she takes in my words, and for some reason, I know she's trying to work it all out in her mind. She begins to tap her pointed nail on the table contemplatively. Rya is smart, top of her class in law school, one of the highest-paid lawyers in her firm, and about to get her dirty-ass dead boss's job.

That's how good she is.

She wins—it's what she's good at.

A simple equation like this will make her realize that she hasn't run far enough away to escape Daddy's influence.

The waitress returns and places a plate of vegetables in front of her, but she makes no move to eat. Instead, she is looking at me.

"You're lying." Her voice is soft. My cock twitches. All the venom has drained from her spiteful mouth, leaving behind something vulnerable. Something I need to break.

"Am I?" I ask, cutting another piece of my steak.

"I won't marry you."

"Oh, but you will." I smile at her.

"No! I *won't*." She pushes back her chair with a loud scrape and doesn't even turn to look back at me as she walks out.

I don't chase women.

But this one may need to be chased.

CHAPTER 6

Rya

My phone dings, and I ignore it.

I find my father's phone number and press call. I don't care what the time is there, I need answers.

"Rya." His voice is pleasant, which is nice on the ear.

"Do you have someone watching me?" I whisper into the phone as I walk the streets. It's dark, and I know I shouldn't be walking back to my apartment alone, but I can't seem to stop myself from doing it. My head is spinning, trying to piece all the facts together. And I'm so fucking angry my blood is boiling.

"Rya, what are you talking about?"

"I just had a meeting with Crue," I inform him.

"Crue?" he asks. "Monti?" I hear the hesitation in his voice.

"Yes," I reply while turning down a dark street.

"He told you this?"

"Yes," I answer, walking a little faster. *Why didn't I get in a fucking cab?*

"I'm sorry," is all he says.

"Are you saying it's true?" I whisper, coming to an abrupt stop in the middle of the sidewalk.

"I couldn't let you go by yourself. I had to protect you."

"Protect me?" I respond, confused. I moved to New York because no one would know who I was, and I wouldn't need protection there. "I haven't known Monica the whole time I've been here."

"I know. There was someone else before her. I knew you were getting suspicious, so I went the safest route..." He pauses. "A friend."

Fury overtakes me like a volcano about to erupt. All this time, I thought I'd been free. Instead, I'd been so, what? Naïve? "I *don't* need *protecting*!" I scream into the phone.

"You do if he's there," he whispers.

I hear my stepmother say something in the background, but I don't wait to hear what else this man has to say. I hang up and grip my phone a little harder than necessary before I walk to the end of the street, where there's more light.

"I can't work out if you're dumb or you think you're lucky."

I jump at the voice coming from behind me. Spinning around, I find Crue stalking toward me. What I assume to be his car waits at the other end of the road. He steps closer, and I step back.

"Walking by yourself at night seems like a gamble." Another step closer and then another, his boots clicking against the pavement. Goose bumps tickle my skin. He stops, but only briefly, to look me up and down. "Do you think yourself better than everyone else?" he asks.

"What the fuck?"

He's directly in front of me now, and I take another step back, my body hitting the cold brick wall behind me. "If you don't shift back, I'll knee you in the balls again. Get the fuck away from me."

"So fiery. I like it."

"Get. Away. From. Me," I repeat with more spirit, punctuating each word before I lift my knee, but he dodges it. I raise my hand to slap him, but he's ready for me and catches it. Then, just as quickly, he snatches the other one and pins them against the wall behind me. Crue moves in until our bodies touch, and I can no longer get my knee up between us to do any damage.

The asshole has me trapped.

"I told you when you were sixteen, I would marry you."

"We were kids. Grow up," I spit back.

"My words hold meaning and truth. From then and until now, I meant it."

"Who would want to marry someone who hates them?" I seethe.

He chuckles and leans in, his lips near my neck. My body shivers, and I know he notices it.

"You don't hate me, not yet anyway."

"That's because I don't know you."

"But *I* know *you*."

"You know facts about me, not who I actually am." I try to push him off, which only makes our bodies press closer together.

That was a mistake.

"Tell me who you are."

"I am a woman who *hates* to be manhandled. Now, get the fuck off of me." From the conversation with my father to now, my blood is lava, rage coming to the forefront.

"No," he says, not moving an inch. "Tell me you'll marry me."

"No," I throw back at him.

When he doesn't move, I can feel myself becoming angrier and angrier, not just because he has me trapped, and I absolutely hate to be trapped, but because I kind of like it.

My body betrays any rational thought.

Not that I would ever admit that to him.

So I do what I know to get out of this situation. His face is close, and I lean forward before I can talk myself out of it. And he, being absolutely arrogant, leans closer, thinking I'm going to kiss him.

Ha.

Not happening.

Opening my mouth, I snap it shut when I reach his cheek and bite down. Hard. Not enough to tear his skin off, but enough that he gets it and moves back.

He grunts, and I feel him harden beneath me.

What the fuck?

Crue pulls back and I can see my teeth imprinted on his face, my pink lipstick also smeared on his cheek.

"Feisty little princess, aren't we?" He smirks, and that only makes me madder. I go in for another bite, this time aiming for his lips—stupid, I know—but they're directly in front of me. If he's going to treat me like a caged wild animal, then that's how I'm going to act.

My phone starts ringing, but we ignore it as he drops me and steps back. I almost fall forward but manage to catch myself. As soon as I'm free, I wipe my mouth and glare up at him. "I hate you," I growl, and he simply smirks.

"That's okay. They say hate sex is amazing. Would you care to try that out right here?"

"Fuck you," I hurl the words out before I turn and march off.

I hear him chuckle as I leave.

And all that does is make me want to go back and knee him again right between the legs.

Asshole.

CHAPTER 7
Crue

"D id she just bite you?" Dominic asks as he studies me.

The damn woman ran off, and I stood there, wondering if I should follow. But I've already chased her once tonight, and even that's testing my limits. And besides, there was something delicious in her fleeing—I will catch her later like a game of cat and mouse—even if she had drawn a little blood.

"Were you watching?" I ask. I told him to stay in the car. Dominic obviously didn't listen.

"Of course. Wait until I tell Angel." He laughs as we walk back to the car. "Oh, by the way, Angel still wants to visit Rya. So just let her."

"Angel can wait," I tell him. "I don't need her ruining this."

"I'm pretty sure you're doing a great job on your own," Dominic adds, and I want to punch him in the face. He holds up his hands and shakes his head. "How long do you plan to live here? It's already been years."

"I don't plan to return to Italy," I inform him, and his eyes widen.

"You have to."

"One day. Maybe."

"The families—" he starts.

I cut him off. "I have the power. You know this. If one of the families chooses to go against that, you know my orders."

"Kill them," he replies.

"Exactly."

"You're stirring up trouble here with the gangs." Dominic pulls open the car door and gets in, and I climb into the passenger seat as he starts the car.

"Trouble is what I'm here for. Some of them have had their seats here because of who their families are. Some aren't worth it, so I'm taking it back."

"You already have most of it back."

"Not all. Some think it's smart to disobey me. Or they try to manipulate it their way." I drop my head from side to side, cracking it.

"You killed all their bosses..." He pauses. "I think they get the message."

I press my thumb to my cheek and draw back smears of pink lipstick, almost impressed. I didn't think the princess would be willing to get her hands dirty.

"What would you do if someone killed me?" I ask.

"I would hunt them down and destroy them," Dominic replies without hesitation.

"Exactly. Some of these families have been raised with the same values, granted they adapted to the American culture. But family? Well, they believe in that, at the very least. And I just tore it all open." I've been here a few years, taking back our family's power. Many years ago, before I was born, my great-grandfather sent family here. They settled in New York and were given money to take over the streets and businesses. But somewhere along the way they became greedy and thought they could take over all of it without any backlash.

Little did they know, I'm hungrier for it than all of them combined.

I hold all the titles.

They are passed down through generations.

I was trained from a young age to be ruthless.

And ruthless is what I will be.

Even against a little princess.

CHAPTER 8
Rya

Dear Miss Ricci
Do you think you would bite like that in
the bedroom?
Reply.
Crue

For fuck's sake.

Members of the board stare back at me expectantly as I put my phone away. I've received emails from Crue since this morning and immediately deleted them. I've been in meetings all day. It's an absolute shit show. With no official manager, other board members have stepped in with how we should manage the press and who should temporarily be in charge.

Now all eyes are on me.

When they offered me the position earlier today, I thought they were kidding. I quickly told them I needed to think about it, which is unlike me. This is what I've been working toward and why I've become the best. But I also feel uncomfortable at the thought that I only received an offer for this position because of *him*. And killing my boss is nothing I want any part of.

"Did you go over the written statement?" Mr. Luca asks me. He's only a few years older than me and has recently taken his father's spot on the board.

"I made a few amendments, and it's ready to be released." Officially, it was a closed case by the police, but as a law firm that defends some of the most high-profile criminals, we're expected to uphold a front. We've made enemies before, but little do they know that the specific criminal in question is also trying to put a ring on my finger. *Ridiculous.*

"So cases will go on as normal, effective immediately," Mr. Luca announces. "Have Kora's and Matthew's clients redistributed to the interns." Two of our lawyers, who had been at my party, quit this morning, too scared that the very same thing that happened to Brian might happen to them.

My phone buzzes in my pocket again, and I hide my frustration.

I swear to God, if he's sent me another email...

"Dismissed," Mr. Luca says, and unofficially, it sounds like he might be the new temporary boss. I collect my files, irritated by my buzzing phone. When I finally retrieve it, I realize that Monica is trying to call again. And like all the other times she's called, I ignore her. I'm not sure if she knows I know, but I have to calm myself before I talk to her so I don't pull something my father would do and kill her.

Because I want to strangle her with my bare hands right now for lying to me.

"Rya." One of my colleagues, Samantha, calls me over. "It looked intense in there," she says, referring to the boardroom.

"It was," I reply. We have only ever spoken a few times, as idle chitchat isn't something I waste much time on at work.

"Is it true?" she whispers as she glances around us, ensuring no one can hear.

My eyebrows furrow. "Is what true?"

"You know. That Brian got shot at your birthday party, and you know the killer? Apparently, he's super-hot."

My sharp gaze cuts to hers. I should've expected as

much, but I don't appreciate idle gossip and being linked to the criminal personally. But what irks me more is how she spoke about him.

"You should know better than to objectify criminals sexually."

She shrinks into herself. "Sorry, I just—"

"But, yes, we'd met once in passing. That's all. I have no idea his reasons for what he did, but the police have closed the case," I say, offering her my sharpest smile.

"Oh, that makes sense," she says politely before quickly finding herself busy with work again. Had it been any other criminal it might've been easier to avoid gossip. But Crue's too bold and uncaring of anyone who might have seen him that night. And I must keep our connection as far away as possible in case others start digging up my past. Because then I won't have any chance of making it on my own, instead relying on my father's name.

My phone pings again as I walk to my office.

I open the email...

Dear Miss Ricci
Don't you know it's bad form to not

reply? I'd hate to have to do anything
drastic to gain your attention.
Reply.
Crue

... AND DELETE IT, furious.

CHAPTER 9

Rya

The week was a spiral of questions, transitions, and court cases, and still, I haven't gotten any closer to accepting the new role I was offered. In truth, I only want to focus on my biggest case to date with the Torrisi family. And my current client seriously fucked up this week. I'd told him to lie low, and instead, he went on another killing spree with some damning evidence that makes my life a living hell to defend. But I will. I'll get him off like I did the others.

Arriving home from work, I spot Monica waiting at the entrance to my building. She's dressed in her usual colorful clothes, and when she sees me, she smiles. After the shit I went through this week at the office, I don't need this, but I suppose there's no avoiding it now.

Monica tries to hug me, but I hold out my hand.

She looks baffled and steps back, arms hanging by her sides. "I've been trying to call and message you all week," she says, a little annoyed. "I thought something had happened to you after last weekend."

Now, it just makes me mad. *Does she actually give a shit?*

"Did you?"

"Don't put that lawyer face on for me. You forget I know you."

"Do you?" I ask. "Know me, I mean." I lift my sunglasses from my eyes and slide them to the top of my head.

"What's with the attitude? Damn, Rya." She pulls back from me and shakes her head.

"I find it funny how you can stand here and pretend. Did you take acting lessons?"

"Acting lessons? What are you on about?"

And then, when I stare at her, her eyes widen with understanding.

"I know," is all I say. "I know."

"Look, let's talk about it. Please." Her usual cheerful tone seems almost desperate.

"You aren't even going to deny it?"

"No. You already know. And I know once you have facts, you will run with them."

"I do because facts never lie. Unlike you."

"Wow, okay." She glances around before she focuses back on me. "At least let me explain. Will you give me that?"

"Don't you think you've had multiple opportunities to do that?" I question. "Like years," I tack on.

"Fine. Okay. I get it. You're mad. And you're allowed to be. But I want you to know that, no matter what, I truly think of you as a friend."

"One who was getting paid, though, right?"

"It wasn't like that."

"Were you or were you not getting paid to be my friend?" I ask again.

She hesitates, then quietly replies, "Yes, I was."

Well, that is my answer.

"Lose my number and never contact me again." I turn, and the doorman opens the door for me. "Ban her from my approved guest list," I tell him, and he nods.

I don't bother looking back as I hurry to the elevator and head to my apartment. I stroll straight for the liquor cabinet, pouring a generous glass of red wine and taking a swig out of the bottle for good measure. I flick off my heels, fall onto my sofa, and turn on the television. Right now, I need to do something mindless. It wouldn't be smart for me to work.

I'm too mad, and I may fuck something up, and I cannot afford to do that. Especially with all the heat on our firm this week.

I have people depending on me.

My phone rings. And rings. Eventually, I reach for it and put it on 'Do Not Disturb.'

But before I realize I'm doing it, I'm already reading my emails.

His name pops up.

Multiple times.

I hate him.

And as I go to throw my phone down, I can't help myself because I want to see what he says, what he's doing.

And why is he still emailing me when I told him I wouldn't marry him?

Because I won't.

He can go fuck himself.

Dear Miss Ricci

Do you remember I know where you live?

Reply.

Crue.

"Arrghh!" I scream at his email. Is this asshole threatening me now? I was certain that saying *"I won't marry you"* was as clear as *"I'm not interested, now fuck off."*

My phone dings in my hand, indicating another email has come through.

Dear Miss Ricci
Knock, knock.
Open the door.
Crue.

My hands clench around my phone. He's joking, right? There is no way he is actually here. And that's when I hear it.

Knock. Knock.

On my apartment door.

I freeze, but then it comes again.

Knock. Knock.

Getting up and walking to the kitchen, I grab

whatever I can find as a weapon, which just so happens to be a pair of sharp scissors, and I quietly move to the door. I look through the peephole to see Crue standing on the other side.

"I can hear you breathing, princess."

This guy is out of his goddamn mind. I huff out a breath and pull open the door.

Crue's gaze catches mine before it falls to what's in my hand. "Do you plan to stab me?" he asks with a raised brow.

"Yes," I reply without hesitation.

"Now, that's no way to treat your future husband," he scolds, sending a shiver racking through me. This guy has a one-track mind. I don't know whether to be impressed by his laser focus or annoyed by his inability to take a damn hint.

"I won't marry you," I all but growl out.

He steps forward, and I lift my hand, holding the scissors. He plucks them from my fingers before I can do anything. Scanning his face, I see my bite mark still decorating his cheek.

"Drinking without me, princess?" He walks in without an invite as if he owns the apartment, scissors in his hand. I stare after him as he shifts to my kitchen and opens the refrigerator despite the bottle of red wine being in clear sight. When he doesn't find what he's looking for, he turns back to me, where I'm still standing at the door. "You have nothing in your fridge."

"I know that."

"How? Or better yet, why?" He closes the refrigerator and goes for the cupboard, pulling that open next. It feels more like a shakedown than it does him searching for alcohol. When he's met with the same thing, he shakes his head. "Do you starve yourself?"

"No."

"Then where the fuck is your shit?" He throws his hands up, and when he does, his sleeve lifts, and I get a sneak peek of more ink.

He might have barged into my home, but that doesn't mean I have to answer all of his questions.

Changing the subject, I curiously ask, "Why do you have so many tattoos?"

"Why do you have no food?" Crue bites back. He decides to settle on the red wine, picking it up and searching for a glass.

I huff out an irritated sigh. We could go back and forth with this all night.

Time—is something I don't have.

I shut the door and nonchalantly shrug as I pick up my glass and down half of it. I'll need this for my sanity to deal with him.

"I have a date and work a lot, so most of my food is at the office. And I didn't say you could have any of that."

I smugly watch his body go rigid. And I feel rather satisfied that I was defiant with a reminder that I'm not his in any way.

"Where is your date?" he asks, striding over to me and plucking the glass of wine out of my hand, pointedly downing the rest with an arrogant smirk.

"You should leave," I say, offering him a sweet smile.

"We have established I'm not a man you can boss around."

"And we established that I am *not* that woman." I cross my arms over my chest. "Now, leave so I can get ready for my date. You've reminded me that I'm hungry."

If looks could kill.

The beautiful storm that swirls in his eyes is powerful, damning, and cruel.

"I'd strongly suggest you don't go on a date."

"And I strongly suggest you leave." I wave my hand to the door. "Yet here you are, still standing in my apartment."

He's all but crowding me now, but I hold my own. I won't submit to anyone, even if they are a Monti.

"Your father promised you to me long ago," he reminds me.

"That sounds like a you-and-him problem, not mine," I say, taking back the glass, certain that it's about to splinter in his hand any second now.

Suddenly, all that beautiful fury twists into a cruel smile. "Yes, I guess it is." He brushes past me and stops when he gets to the door. I feel my body sag in subtle relief that he's leaving. "Don't suppose you would mind if I had your father killed for not upholding his end of the deal?"

The relief is replaced by a cold dread that washes over me at his words.

Did he really just threaten my father?

No.

No way.

He can't be serious.

Can he?

"You can't," I say.

He pulls the door open and walks out but turns back to say, "I'd suggest you ask your father who I am, then tell me *I can't*." His smile is a violent promise before he closes the door behind him. That cold terror grips me only briefly before I remember who my father is, and I remember he can look after himself. But I find myself picking up my phone and calling my father anyway for a discussion. He answers after the second ring.

"Sweetie," he answers cheerfully.

"Crue Monti. How dangerous is he?" I exclaim.

A deliberate silence, then, "Why are you asking?"

"Because he just left my apartment. Please tell me."

I hear him curse under his breath and that's never a good sign. "He puts us old folk to shame. He is ruthless. Couldn't care less who he kills. Or why."

"You promised me to him."

"How—" He stops again. Did he really think I didn't know after all these years? Sure, I'd overheard it in small talk and in passing—and I'd heard it directly from Crue himself—but I thought I'd laid that to rest when I didn't marry at eighteen, and it wasn't brought up ever again.

The silence on the other end of the line concludes that, obviously, my father had the same impression. But I know him better than that. If the Monti family expected their agreement to be kept, he'd fulfill it— even at my expense.

"I won't marry him," I state, then hang up. I clutch my phone in my hand as I pace back and forth.

I don't intend to marry him.

I never want to be married to anyone.

Marriage and children are not part of my plan.

All I have ever wanted is freedom to do what I want when I want.

And I have that.

That is until Crue walked back into my life.

I'm contemplating right now if I should even go on this date. But it's been planned for so long, and I have already canceled on this man twice before. I can't do it a third time. I like him. Okay *like* might be a bit of a stretch, but I could potentially see a good time in the bedroom. I have needs, and sometimes my toys just don't cut it. And I definitely need some distraction to take the edge off after this week.

Crue won't kill my father.

Will he? Surely not.

I watch the time go by and contemplate canceling.

I should.

But why am I letting a man dictate my life?

I absolutely should not.

It's what he wants and the furthest thing from what I want. So, instead, I pour another glass of wine, determined to show this prick who I really am. I'm not a doll to be told what to do.

I can fuck whoever I want.

CHAPTER 10

Crue

I duck just in time.

When I turn around, I see Angel with her hands on her hips, staring daggers at me. Her belly is large with her pregnancy.

"I want to see her. Stop being an asshole and let me see her." She reaches for another object to throw at me, and Dominic steps in just in time, grabbing it from her.

"You can't throw shit at him," he tells her, and she looks past him to glare at me.

"I will cut your throat in your sleep, you asshole. Let me see her."

"Fucking hell," Dominic mutters and turns back to look at me. "She didn't mean it."

"Oh, but I did." Angel hits him. "Don't you dare speak for me."

"Woman, you can't threaten him." He shakes his head. "I'll talk to him." Dominic tries to touch her face to calm her down, but she pushes his hand away, grabs something else, and throws it over his shoulder so it just misses me.

"I have plans to see her tonight," I tell Angel. "She's on a date, one I specifically suggested she *not* go on."

Angel pauses, looks at me, and smiles. "She isn't going to listen to you. You get that, right?" Angel smirks.

"I don't intend for her to. I have to teach her first. So once she thinks her date went amazing, I'll kill him and maybe send her some body parts to remind her who *the fuck* I am."

"Best way to run her off for good, I'd say." Angel flips her hair over her shoulder, then turns and walks away.

Dominic stands there, his hands threading through his hair. "Well, shit. Sorry, man. I didn't think..." He shakes his head. "Do you plan to kill Rya's date?"

"Yep." I tap my phone to bring up the video feed I hacked into from her building. She's standing at the entrance, and some guy in a suit is leaning in as he talks to her, a smile on his face. She turns to go back in but stops. "Do not do it!" I growl to her image on the screen. She mouths something and then shakes her head while he watches her with keen interest. I don't blame him. Does this fucking woman have a bad angle?

"Maybe you shouldn't watch," Dominic suggests, peering over my shoulder at my phone.

She stretches out her hand, and he takes it and steps through the doorway, closing the door behind them.

"Well, shit!" My brother steps back. "Okay, let's be calm about this. Think rationally. I mean, you killed her boss not just because of his dirty work but because you found out he was taking inappropriate photos and recordings of her. But this is different... it's consensual."

"It wasn't just her he was recording," I tell him. And I didn't have to explain that my soon-to-be wife isn't in a position where she could suggest or offer consent to any other man.

"Yep, sure. You killed him because he had a camera in the women's bathroom. For the protection of the other women." He rolls his eyes at the last bit. "But he only really seemed to store her content."

"Scum," I say as I pocket my phone. "I'm going out."

"Maybe you shouldn't," Dominic says. Two of my men, who are standing outside the door, nod and then flank me as I leave. "Crue!" Dominic yells.

I don't listen. What's the point of listening when I know exactly what I plan to do?

No one can change my mind. In all my years, no one has been able to do that. So why would that change now?

"Get me all you can on this man," I order one of my men, who is sitting in the passenger seat of the car. I airdrop him the photograph as the driver takes us back to her apartment.

My little defiant vixen.

Little does she know, she's playing with fire.

And when I want something, I get it.

Even if they put up a fight.

CHAPTER 11

Rya

Andrew's hands are everywhere. Literally everywhere on me. It's like someone put him on fast-forward, and he forgot how to slow down.

Like, do your hands need to be there?

I take a deep breath and try not to think of another man while this man is trying and failing to undress me.

But it's hard.

The way Crue's eyes zoom in on me is like... it's as if he can see straight through my bullshit and calls me out on it every damn time.

Asshole.

"Andrew."

He pauses but just as quickly removes his grabby hands from me and starts with his own clothes.

Andrew smiles like he's won the lottery as he unbuttons his shirt.

"Slow down. It's not a race," I tell him, then turn and enter the kitchen. I open the cabinet, grab a bottle of red wine, and pour myself a glass. When I look up, I see him still undressing. "Do you want a glass?"

"I want *you*," he says eagerly.

I laugh a little. I mean, it's nice to be wanted. And Andrew knows why he's here. To fuck. He knows I want nothing more, that sex is it for me. And he agreed. So why am I not letting him get to it? Lifting my glass of wine to my lips, I drink the whole thing and shake my head.

"You want me."

Okay, he wants me.

I can do this.

I love sex, and sex loves me.

I step around the kitchen counter to find a naked Andrew waiting for me.

Sex.

It's just sex.

"Why do you want me?" I ask, reaching for my half-unbuttoned shirt that Andrew was attempting to get off of me.

"Have you seen yourself?" he asks with a smile, his cock hardening even further when my gaze drops to it.

It's a nice size, average, maybe. He has confidence, I must say that.

I met Andrew a few months ago through Monica, and we've been messaging and talking for a bit. I haven't had time or the chance to go out with him until tonight. And I was about to cancel on him again, but Crue made me mad.

Why should *he* get a say on who I date?

He shouldn't.

He's known me for what? A day or two? And he thinks he has full control of me.

Now that's a laugh and a half. Crue could never have control of me.

I would never sign up for that.

Unbuttoning the last few buttons of my shirt, I pull it off, leaving me in a skirt and a red lacy bra. His gaze roams my body, and I know he appreciates what he sees.

His hardness shows me what he's thinking.

Andrew steps toward me, but I put up a finger, halting him. "Skirt on?" I ask.

"Off," he says without hesitation.

I smirk and unzip it before shimmying the material down my legs and letting it drop to the floor. I'm standing in my red lacy set with matching stockings, garters, and heels. I turn around and feel him come up behind me just before his hands brush my ass. He rubs circles on my flesh, and I feel his cock ever so close to me. "I want to bend you over."

"Hmm, what else?" I wait for him to speak, but his hands disappear, and I hear a loud crack before it sounds like something falls. Looking over my shoulder, I don't see Andrew. The person staring back at me is the man I wish would touch me. My gaze lowers, and I find Andrew on the floor at his feet.

"What have you done?" I ask, stepping back, my eyes trained on Andrew.

Who is not moving.

I drop down and crawl toward him, my hand reaching to touch his neck. With shaky fingers, I check his pulse. When I don't feel anything, I look up at Crue watching me.

"You are so beautiful on your hands and knees."

"What did you do?" I whisper, unable to look away from him. He's dressed in the same suit he left here only a few hours ago. He bends, his finger lifting my chin so I don't break our stare.

"You are mine! In every sense of the word." I shake my head, and he leans in and touches his lips to mine. I'm paralyzed, unable to move. *How can this be? How can he do this to me? And why do his lips taste like my favorite treat?* His tongue slides into my mouth, and I pull back, falling backward on my ass as I look at Andrew.

Crue stays crouched, and the angle makes him seem more predator than man. "You will learn to listen to me."

His words make me angry. Not just angry for Andrew, who I'm guessing is dead, but for what he's implying.

"I am *not* yours." I spit the words at him.

Crue laughs and stands, and I sit there as he calmly goes to the door and opens it. "If any of you look at her, I will pick your eyeballs from your sockets," he says to someone in the hallway.

"Yes, sir." Two men enter the apartment, dressed in hazmat suits. I watch in complete horror as they walk over to Andrew, roll him up, pick him up, and walk out. Not once do they look at me. I glance down at my body and remember what I am wearing. I stand quickly, and Crue is next to me in an instant, his hands around my waist and his body pressed against mine.

"Princess, are you going somewhere?"

My first reaction is to get away from him. Far, far away from him. But he has a hold of me. And our bodies are pressed tightly against one another.

"Let me go."

"Say please," he whispers in my ear. A shiver racks

through me. His hands are on my bare back, resting just above my ass, and I can feel his excitement pressing into me.

And I hate that I like it.

A loud thump makes me jump, and I manage to push back and out of his grasp. The door closes, and only the two of us are in here now.

"How did you get in?" I ask as I try to cover my body with my arms.

His eyes scan me with a devilish gleam. "I let myself in," he replies, not once breaking eye contact. "It's what husbands do."

"You are *not* my damn husband!" I yell at him.

"Yet." He winks with a half-cocked smile.

Oh my God. I turn away from Crue and can feel his gaze on my ass. "Stop looking," I call out over my shoulder.

"But I can't, it's so... delicious. I want to imprint on it."

"In your wildest fucking dreams," I shout as I reach my room and pull on a robe. Taking a deep breath, I try to gather myself. I don't even know what to do about this man. He keeps on inserting himself into my life without my permission. I'm not going to lie, he's very nice to look at, but he is also fucking crazy. And I try to stay away from crazy as much as possible.

I've been trying to lead a simple life since I left home. I was always surrounded by guards and had to attend so many events. At least here, I don't have to answer to anyone. And how the fuck do I explain the Andrew situation? I suppose there is no explanation, considering how quickly they rolled him out like he was nothing. Meant nothing. And although we weren't close, that shit is absolutely fucking crazy.

"My face is getting better, in case you were wondering." I turn to find him at my bedroom door.

"I wasn't. Now, leave."

"So, about your father..."

I approach him, my finger pointing in his face as I clench my teeth. I've had about enough of this asshole pushing his weight around. And if he thought killing my boss and then Andrew was going to force me into submission, he has another thing coming.

"If you ever threaten to kill my father... actually, fuck that, anyone in my family, I will bite your cock off. Do you feel me? Asshole." His dark eyes lock on mine, and his tongue slides along the back of his teeth as he sucks air, my finger still pointing in his face as anger radiates through me.

Who does he think he is?

Before I can do anything, or before he even replies, his mouth opens and he takes my finger inside. I feel his tongue slide around it before he pulls off and smacks his lips. *Did he just suck my finger?* I'm so flabbergasted that I stand here, looking between my finger and his mouth.

He didn't, surely.

But he did.

"I'll take your words into consideration. Now, I would highly recommend you don't go on another date." Crue turns and heads for the door. "Next time, wear black." He winks before he disappears.

And I'm left standing here wondering what the fuck just happened.

CHAPTER 12

Rya

"You do realize that little stunt you pulled will make it even harder to secure your case, right? I told you to lie low."

The delinquent with a mohawk shrugs. He has a mixture of fading colored ink all over his body. We sit in my office, me and this shithead I have to represent. I look at his uncle, Andreas Torrisi, as a voice of reason. He seems even more furious than I am. Good. At least someone in this family understands the magnitude of what he's done.

Matteo, who is no more than twenty years old, looks between me and his uncle. Under pressure, he throws his hands up in defeat and points at me. "What? She's the best! And even you said the little dealers on the corner were becoming a problem for business, so I took care of them."

I blow out a whistle as Andreas covers his face with his hands. "Not while you're in the middle of a trial, you dumbass."

I lean back in my chair and cross my arms over my chest. Shit, Crue might have been bold, but at least he was a little more calculating than this shithead. I raise the blurred image from the street surveillance camera. At least he kept his head low and had a hat on, but it's still unnecessary fuel for those who are trying to put this shithead behind bars for killing their son.

"Is this the only evidence you think they currently have?"

He shrugs again and looks between me and his uncle. "What? I don't know. I think so." Silence fills the room. "Well, you're the best, aren't you? You can still get me off, can't you?"

I look at Andreas, my jaw tightening.

"Do you realize how much you're costing me? I might be tempted to throw your ass in jail myself after all of this." Andreas grabs him by the back of the neck and hoists him up as if he is nothing but a young pup. "Leave us for a moment."

Matteo eyes us once more before begrudgingly leaving the room. Andreas watches him the whole time. "He hasn't exactly been the same since his father was killed a year ago."

I roll my shoulders and reposition myself, my back straighter as he sits across from me. I really don't care if this meeting extends, considering the minutes that roll by add to my bankroll. I'm more than happy to listen, but not for too long.

"I heard something interesting," he says. "I heard that the man who shot down your boss was a Monti."

I clasp my hands together, casually resting them in front of my face. "And here I thought I was being paid to ensure your nephew doesn't go to prison. I didn't know gossip was something the Torrisi family likes to entertain."

He chuckles at that with a rueful grin. And that's when I'm reminded of the type of men I work with— those who underestimate me because I'm a woman. They expect answers when questioned. I'll be fucked if I'm going to let someone interrogate me in my own office.

He wags his fat finger at me. "You're a smart woman. I'm sure you know not to get caught up with the wrong type of criminals."

"It's not my job to differentiate between tier levels of crime and ego. Only who's signing my next paycheck." I stare at him over my knuckles and plaster on an insincere smile. "An official statement went out at the start of the week. The criminal is already in jail."

"I heard he was killed on his first day there," Andreas says.

That's news to me.

"Well, looks like you know more about it than I do," I say. "I look forward to seeing you in our next court meeting," I add dismissively.

He rolls his tongue in his cheek with a tight, arrogant smirk. Men like this think they can buy anything or anyone. I don't shift my gaze or tight smile.

A low knock on the door interrupts us. Andreas nods and opens the door, where Mr. Luca waits. He looks between us, the tension palpable.

"Have a lovely evening, Miss Ricci," Andreas says as he exits my office.

"Is everything okay?" Mr. Luca asks once Andreas is gone.

I look over my white knuckles at him. "It's fine. How can I help you, Mr. Luca?" I ask, now packing up the last of my items. A few of us are going out for a drink after work to celebrate a closed case that had been worked on over the last year and cost me most of my free time.

He closes the door behind him. "I just wanted to know if you'd thought any more about the new role."

My hand freezes for a moment before I continue packing. "I thought the board was giving me a month to decide."

"They are, but I thought you would've jumped at the opportunity. I've watched you for years. You're ruthless in court and the very best at what you do. So why the hesitation? Do you have concerns that what happened to Brian might happen to you?"

A tense laugh escapes me before his eyebrows crease in confusion. "Sorry," I say, shaking my head. If only he knew what type of woman I really am. "No, I don't think I'm going to get gunned down." *Maybe any other male I look at twice will, though.* "I just need to shuffle a few things around, that's all." *And shuffle a certain someone out of my life.*

"Okay. I just wanted to make sure," he says, seemingly unconvinced. "If you need anything, you'll let me know. Yes?"

"Of course." I nod, somewhat irritated. Why is he scrutinizing me? We didn't have much involvement prior to this. Sure, he has shares in the firm, but there isn't any need to check up on me personally. "If that's all you need, I'm going to join the others," I say, walking past him. He moves out of the way, leaving the room so I can lock my office door behind me.

"Have a good evening," he offers before walking away.

I feel the ping of my phone in my suit jacket.

I pull it out and read the email.

Dear Miss Ricci

I've been unable to stop thinking about you on your hands and knees. It's been rather distracting, and I hope you'll take responsibility for such matters.

P.S. Red is the only other color besides black you should wear.

Reply.

Crue

ASSHOLE.

CHAPTER 13

"I don't care what you say... I'm coming," Angel says as she forces herself into my car. Dominic swears from the front seat as she does. "I know you're going to see her. It's been what? A week? And I can tell you're having withdrawals because your killings have doubled."

I look at Dominic and eye him through the rearview mirror.

"What? She knows everything."

"Only because you fucking tell her," I yell.

Angel rubs her belly as she sits next to me. If she weren't pregnant right now, I would throw her out of this car myself. "I don't have withdrawals. To me, women are a means to an end. They are there to lie on their back and fall pregnant." Angel laughs in a half-crazed hyena pitch. "Dominic." I grind my teeth.

"You expect her to have your kids, and what? Marry you as well?" Angel asks. "You're barking up the wrong tree. You do know I still talk to her, right?"

"Of course we do. Your phones are tapped." Her eyes widen, and she reaches to the front and hits Dominic.

"Why didn't you tell me that?"

"I don't listen. It's just in case anyone ever tries to threaten you," he explains, trying to appease her. When in reality it's because I like listening to Rya speak. I had to decide if I wanted to go after her, and it took me years to decide. But somehow, without her even knowing, she got under my skin, and when I saw her for the first time again, there was no going back.

She *is* the woman I am going to marry.

"I listen," I tell her with a grin.

"I hate you," she grumbles, and I merely smile.

We come to a stop outside a bar. I spot Rya seated inside with a few of her work colleagues, mostly men, and before we can say anything, Angel is out of the car and heading inside.

"Can you try to be nicer to her?" Dominic asks.

I raise a brow at him. "What?" I say as if I didn't hear him correctly.

"She's pregnant with your niece."

"And?"

"You treat her so awful." He shakes his head.

"I treat her like a sister. How else would you like me to treat her? If she were any other person talking to me the way she does, you know for a fact they would not be breathing." I turn toward the bar's window and see Rya happy, with a large smile as she hugs Angel. Dominic and I stay there for a few minutes to watch the two women interact.

"I love her," Dominic says.

"Love is dumb. It will get you killed."

"So what is it with Rya, then?"

I don't hesitate when I answer, "Obsession." I smile. I wonder if I fucked her enough, if she would be out of my system or stuck there for life.

I'd been thinking about her all day in those tight, lacy red pieces, and it had driven me half mad.

I guess there is only one way to find out.

CHAPTER 14
Rya

At first, I think I'm seeing things because not only is Angel here, but she is heavily pregnant. I am shocked. Knowing about a heavily pregnant Angel and seeing a heavily pregnant Angel are two different things.

Her arms automatically go around me, and she pulls me from my chair. I awkwardly hug her back, the height difference obvious, especially when I'm in my four-inch heels. She doesn't say anything as we hug, but I can feel her crying as she holds me. I rub her back and wait for her to calm down, and when I think she's finally about to let go, she squeezes me a little bit tighter, her round belly pushing against me.

Eventually, she starts to calm down.

Pulling back, I look down at her.

"You're here." I lift my hand and wipe away her tears. She smiles and swipes at both eyes with her hands, smudging her mascara.

"Sorry. I'm so sorry. I tried to come see you so many times."

"It's okay, you're here now. I mean, how did you know I was here, though?" I ask, confused. I never told anyone I was coming here, yet she walked in like she knew I would be there. We'd been trying to organise a catch-up time but everything had fallen through so far this week.

"Him," she says and throws her thumb over her shoulder. I look up just in time to see the door open, and Crue walk in. People stare, then just as quickly, they avert their gazes. I'm here with a few work colleagues who were at my party that night. Which means they would have seen him and what he did. Some start to move away while I remain standing in place as he walks closer. *Shit, this is bad.* Seeing us together once could be considered a coincidence but seeing us together twice is problematic.

Crue looks to the man standing to my left. Matthew, who has worked on a few cases with me.

"You know who I am?" Crue asks, to which Matthew nods his head. Crue glances behind me to where a few other colleagues are. "You all know who I am?"

"Yes," they say in eerie unison.

Does he think he's God?

"Good. I'm pleased to hear you all kept your mouth shut." He motions to the bartender. "A round for the bar." I turn to see everyone wearing wary expressions, their heads cocked to the side trying to listen in or their eyes narrowed as if in confusion. How do I take charge of this situation? Do I tell him to leave? Or do I pretend I don't know him? But by the way they're curiously observing him, it's obvious everyone is too scared to ever speak against him in any way. Some great law firm we are. When I shift my gaze back to the spot where Angel was standing, she's gone and has been replaced by the one person who seems to epically piss me off simply by existing.

"We have to talk," he demands.

"No, we don't." I look past him to see Angel hugging Dominic, his hand immediately gravitating to her stomach.

"Yes, we do. I have your ring."

I am shocked when he pulls out a blue box and flicks it open. I quickly reach over and slam it shut. "You so better not be giving me a fucking ring."

"Anyone told you before that you have a dirty mouth?"

"Anyone told you before that you are an asshole who thinks he can get everything he wants?"

He smirks before leaning in to whisper, "I don't *think* I can. I *know* I can."

"You can't have me," I tell him as I grab my bag from the stool and step around him.

He doesn't reach out to grab me. *Well, at least that's progress.*

Fuck this! I was about to leave anyway. I down the last of my drink and make my way to Angel, who is still with Dominic.

"You want to go get some dessert?" I ask her, and she nods and takes my hand as we walk out.

"He's going to be pissed," Angel says somewhat cheerfully.

"Let him be pissed. I don't care."

"He bought that ring today. Took ages in the jeweler." She mischievously side-glances at me.

"You don't think I will actually marry him, do you?"

"Of course she does," Crue says, coming up behind us.

"Oh my God, *please* leave me the fuck alone." I

wave a hand between us. "This whole stalking thing is next level."

"Have dinner with me, and I will leave you alone. For a while at least."

"You're trying to bribe me to have dinner with you? Didn't we do this song and dance already? It failed, remember?"

"Dinner, and you have my word. I'll leave you alone for a bit."

I have the unnerving feeling that he won't leave us alone if I don't agree, and the only person I want to spend time with right now is my best friend. It fucks me off to realize I can't spend any time with her without what is considered *his* permission. But it's also been so long since I've seen her.

I turn to Angel. "Are you free later?" I ask.

She looks to Crue and then back to me with a nod. "Sure."

I turn to Crue. "Fine, I'll have dinner with you. And then leave me the fuck alone," I say.

"As you wish." He smirks, and almost immediately another sleek black car pulls around the corner and parks at the curb.

I look between the car Dominic has just driven and him. A spark of irritation flutters through me. *The prick knew I'd end up going with him.* "Do you always have men on standby?" I ask dryly, so annoyed at his arrogance.

A cocky smile curves his lips. "And even more women."

An unfamiliar burn sets my stomach alight at the thought of Crue with another woman. I swat it away, wondering how any woman in their right mind could seriously consider falling for this asshole. Then again, with looks like his, he could have anyone.

He adjusts his suit jacket as he opens the door for me. I get in, and he walks around to the other side and slides in next to me. I look out the window to see Dominic blow out a whistle and Angel offer a small wave.

It still blows my mind to see them as this... happy family. After all these years, I knew about them. Not the marriage. But still, seeing it is so different to the sixteen year old friend I'd left behind all those years ago.

"I can't believe they're still together," I say.

"And still insufferably infatuated with one another. It's sickening."

I turn to him and see the disgust on his face. "You don't believe in love?" I question.

"Do you?"

"Possibly," I say, shrugging.

"I don't. It's purely an obsession you have with one another until it dies. Because obsessions always do."

I side-eye him, infuriated by his attractiveness even at this angle. He has his fist closed under his jaw as he watches passersby. Not with curiosity but almost as if he's a king in his domain, irritated that they're in his way.

It's not that I'm surprised the man doesn't believe in love. He obviously doesn't have an ounce of care or kindness in his body. But it's in the venomous way that he says it. A previous sweetheart, perhaps? Maybe even Mommy and Daddy issues. Lord knows we all have them. Of all the criminals I've studied and interacted with, I have the impression he might be the most cruelly cut.

"Take a photo, princess. It lasts longer."

I feel heat flush my cheeks, irritated that my stare lingered so long. And worse, he always seems to know when I'm looking.

The car slows to a stop, and he exits and walks around to my side. Opening the door, he offers me his hand, but I refuse to take it as I climb out and grip my purse to myself.

It still doesn't add up.

All he talks about is marriage.

He's a man who doesn't believe in love and could own the world if he wanted to. So why stalk me?

"So what's the point of marriage?" I ask as he strides into the restaurant, straight past the hostess, and keeps going to a booth in the back. He waves for me to enter, and he sits across from me after I sit. I hate how this was all just so conveniently prepared for us. He knew I would come with him and I find that so infuriating.

"Marriage is just another contract," he says, reaching for the water and pouring us a glass each. "It's a deal between two people, and this arrangement could benefit you wisely. Not only would you have status, but you would be one of the most feared women ever."

"I don't care to be feared unless it's in the courtroom," I inform him. He sits back and takes me in. That cool, harsh gaze on me as if he's deciding what to do with me. "Why am I here?"

He pulls out the box again, placing it on the table between us as the waitress comes over. I take a sharp, constricted breath at the sight of the damn box right in front of me. Just by looking at the box I know this ring cost a small fortune. This fucking box is going to be the death of me. I want to throw it across the room, but if anything, he'll demand I get on all fours to crawl and bring it back to him.

I scan the menu as he orders a steak and waits for me to speak.

"I'll have the green curry buddha bowl, please." When I'm finished, I hand her the menu, but her gaze is on Crue. And his gaze is fixated on me.

"Why no meat?" he asks, effectively dismissing the waitress.

"It's something I decided on many years ago and never went back," I reply, my gaze leaving his face and falling to the box.

"You can open it."

A part of me really wants to, just to look at what he got, knowing it will be stunning. But the other part knows how stupid that would be—to even look at the ring because it would give him hope, which I don't want to give him.

Instead, I meet his gaze again, my disinterest evidence enough that I am not going to play into his game.

"How long have you been in charge? What do you call it these days... a mafia kingpin?" I say with an eye roll.

He quirks an unfriendly smile and leans in. "Your father is a part of us, so why the attitude?" And before I can answer, he raises a brow. "Kingpin?"

I shrug. "Sounded good. Fitting, really."

"I like to just go with 'boss.'" He smirks as the waitress comes back with a bottle of wine. She fills our glasses in silence and places the bottle on the table before she walks off again, obviously offended that he hasn't offered her one ounce of attention since we arrived. And I don't know why, but, for some reason, having this powerful man's undivided attention is nice. Even if he is batshit crazy. *Damn, am I really that desperate to scratch my itch?* I down a mouthful of the wine, desperate for relief from all the menacing ways this man seems to crawl under my skin.

"I'm sure you can marry any woman," I point out and nod to the box.

"It's you I want."

"You don't even know me," I remind him, then take another sip, which he seems to find almost amusing, before he takes a mouthful of his own. "And I don't know you."

"Don't I?" he asks, leaning in.

"All right, hotshot. What's your impression of me then?" Part of me wonders how much I'll regret asking him that question—as if I care what he thinks of me—but I do like to challenge and prove someone wrong.

"You like to win in all aspects of life. You aren't one to divulge too much of your personal life, and Angel can attest to that. You don't ask too many questions unless you require the correct answer. I know I make you nervous."

I roll my eyes at that and take another mouthful, but he continues. "Your lip twitches when you look at me like it's torn between kissing me and yelling profanities." I stare at him. "You just did it again." And now I'm self-conscious. This arrogant, cocky bastard. He picks up his glass and lifts it to his lips. "Do you want to know about me?"

"Not particularly," I answer.

But he proceeds to tell me anyway. "I wasn't chosen for this job. I was born into it. From early on, I was molded to be who I am today. Trained and taught to be what I represent."

"And what is that?"

"Power. Obedience. And profit."

"Classic kingpin," I mock. "Big opinion of yourself and all."

He slowly leans back and assesses me. I doubt many sound off to him like this, and I wonder if my determination to be free of this life makes me lash out. Or maybe it's my inability to let any man in court or out of court try to hold reign over me.

"My father was proud, up until the day I killed him, that is."

"I'm sorry, you what?" I say incredulously. Crue is deadly, matter-of-fact.

"Having the Monti name comes with burdens. Had you stayed around for your own duties, I'm sure you might've understood."

I begin to tap my sharp nail on the table, ready to jump across the surface and strangle this man to death.

He continues, "My father's downfall was that he polished me as a blade so purposefully that when he noticed his men listening to me more than him, Monti name or not, he planned to kill both of his heirs. He was a man not ready to give up his throne when it was already mine."

"I don't believe you," I deny openly. I might have been away from the politics of my father's world, but I know, above all, that family matters. Especially a son.

"It's the truth, princess. I was raised on cruelty, not affection. Affection is something I've never needed and why I've come as far as I have. So that's why I don't need love. I only need marriage. Another contract. One that will equally benefit you." He raises his glass in cheers before taking a sip.

Despite his arrogance, I can't imagine what it must have been like to know that your own father put a hit out on you. My father might have been many things, but he would never have done anything like that.

"I feel sorry for you."

He seems almost confused, that is if he could have such a feeling.

"Your mother didn't love you," he says matter-of-factly. Had I not crossed that realization a long time ago I might have almost been hurt. He's telling me something I already know. My so-called mother has all the traits of a sociopath. She could pretend to care on the outside and mimic social skills so profusely that I'd almost consider her a con woman. But on the inside, she was nothing but a void. Self-serving in every way. Sure, it hurt when I found out about the sizable payments she'd receive from my father regularly for taking me in. But I'd learned to use her to get away from there. So if she profited in the process, good for her.

My father cares, though, despite his hard life and how feared he is. Maybe not to the extent other fathers do, but he still cares. He never showered me with love, though I'm sure Honey gets that. Not from him but from my stepmother. She adores Honey, who never really realizes how lucky she is.

"I didn't need her love, just her support."

"To leave the country," he confirms.

"Yes."

"You see, we are more alike than you think."

"We aren't."

"If you say so." He winks as the food arrives and then goes quiet as we eat. Then he looks over at my plate.

The moment passes and I can't find myself organically able to ask about his mother, who had no mention.

"What do you need for us to get married?" he asks.

I huff out another frustrated breath. For some big-shot kingpin, he certainly sounds a lot like a parrot.

"Why are you so persistent?" I ask.

"Because my alternative is not what I'm after."

"Alternative?"

"Yes. I'm to be married by thirty-four. It's expected. Families are expecting a wedding and an heir."

"And what if you don't fulfill that expectation?" I ask. "You're the boss, as you said. Can't you make new rules?"

He drops his fork and picks up his napkin to wipe his face. "It doesn't work like that. Yes, I could potentially try to avoid it. But, you see, it all moves so smoothly because of business. They expect certain things, and in return, so do I. The drugs that are cooked, the henchmen who look after all the businesses, expect the family to stay strong, and when you go against the grain, that trust is broken.

"We may walk in and kill them for a late payment, but we still have their respect because, in the end, they know what to expect. These are the rules that have been tied to us since before we were born. Powerful families have contracts with us, including yours, who agreed to this. We unite them by marriage. Then, the next generation will go to another powerful family. It's all linked in the grand scheme of things. I'm sure your father has told you."

He's told me pieces. But I never really knew the inner workings of how and why this all had to be. But the moment I found out that I was being married off, I ran with absolute resolve that I wouldn't belong to anyone but myself. And yet, here he sits, the very person wanting to put that collar around my throat, and I don't like that thought one little bit.

"So what happens if I say no again?"

"I *will* be married by the time I'm thirty-four," he states, and that's the only explanation he offers.

CHAPTER 15
Crue

Beautiful and wicked, that's who sits across from me right now.

I watch as she eats her food, lost in her own mind. She does that a lot. Withdraws to think about things, as if she's figuring out some kind of complicated algebra. She taps her pointed, polished nail contemplatively as well. I didn't want to divulge too much to her. Things like that I have listened to her conversations multiple times, and I know *exactly* who she is. And yet, this is a whole new version that only I get to see. This fire in her eyes. The defiant spirit. The sexual torment. I might as well put her on a fucking pedestal because she's doing all of those things to me. Intentionally or not.

I know who she is.

And exactly what she wants.

I don't plan to marry anyone else because only she will do. I had a feeling she would be stubborn. After all, she is Mr. Ricci's daughter, and that man is a hardass. The day I went to his house to tell him I was going after her, he didn't believe me, which was his own stupidity. Really, he should know better by now because I say what I mean and do what I say.

She picks up her wine and takes a sip. I see so much of her father in the defiant expression on her face. She hasn't realized it yet, but she will be one of the greatest assets to ever join this family. Not only is she a powerful lawyer who is incredibly well respected in the criminal world, but she oozes concentrated sophisticated power. She has her head screwed on right, which is probably why she won't agree to marry me. Little does she know the lengths that I will go to make her mine.

"I could give you the world," I tell her.

Rya's gaze flicks back down to the blue box, and I push it closer to her.

"Did you actually think it would work... you showing up and demanding me to marry you?"

"Possibly. I figured you would after I threatened to kill your father."

"So you would what? Get me to marry you on a

threat, then what? You expect me to what exactly? Kiss you? Love you? Fuck you?" She almost chokes on her words.

"Are you telling me you haven't thought about me sliding my hands all over that body?" I see her throat contract on her next sip. "Haven't thought about when I reach between your legs and spread them wide, as I get on my hands and knees and show you what a real dessert is?" Her eyes go wide, and the waitress coughs as she picks up the bottle of wine and pours us another glass.

When she's gone, Rya leans in, composure intact.

"You wouldn't know what to do with me." She smirks.

With a cruel smile, I tell her, "I told you they call me boss."

"And they call me Candy every Saturday night," she says, acting bored.

"Okay, let's make a wager."

"A wager?" she asks, confused. "On what?"

"If I can make you come, you marry me. If I don't, I will leave and not bother you again."

"That's..." She shakes her head. "That's insane."

"I know what I can do and how to please a woman. You'd be putty in my hands." I smirk at her.

"No."

Reaching across the table, I cover her hand with mine and use my fingertip to draw random shapes on the back of it. She watches, her brow furrowed in thought.

Fight or flight. Does she give in to me? Or does she pull back?

"I want to fuck you, princess, and I know you want to fuck me."

"I do not," she says, not pulling her hand away as I continue to draw imaginary images on the back of her hand.

"You never got off that night with... what's his name again?" I pretend to think on it, when in reality, I know exactly who the cocksucker was.

"Andrew," she whispers.

"That's right. You never got off with Andrew. And I know a woman like you needs a release. You planned to fuck him when you needed it, right? No relationship, just sex. Why can't we have that?"

Rya pulls her hand back now, snatching it away and placing it under the table. "Because you want to marry me, that's why."

"So if I told you I didn't want to marry you, I could fuck you?" When she stays silent for a minute longer, I grab the ring box and place it in my pocket. "Done! Your place or mine?"

"I never agreed to it. You are so fucking twisted. How can you expect me to fuck you?"

"Preferably on your back so I can watch those fucking eyes water as you come." I wave my hand in the air to get the waitress's attention, then give her my credit card when she approaches the table.

I stand and offer Rya my hand. She shakes her head with a tight smile. Polite enough if anyone were watching, but the venom in her tone is purely for me to hear when she says, "I am *not* fucking you."

"But you are." I lean in closer. "No more marriage talk. That's the deal."

"No."

"Okay." I pull the ring back out and drop down to one knee. Her face goes red, and people gush at me, starting to whisper.

Reaching for me, she grits out, "Get up."

"Which option?" I go to open the box.

She snaps it shut. "I *won't* marry you."

"So you'll fuck me?"

"You know this is a really weird way to try to seduce someone," she whispers.

"The people are waiting for an answer."

She quickly scans the restaurant before her gaze comes back to me. "Stand up."

"Which option?"

"For fuck's sake." She shakes her head and attempts to walk off, but I capture her wrist and pull her back.

"Which option?"

"I can still knee you in the balls," she says with a satisfied smirk.

"Is the thought of fucking me that bad for you?" I ask. I know it's not, but I'm waiting to see how honest she is.

"I-I..." I stand at her stutter.

"We're fucking," I say with finality.

Rya tries to step back, but I still have her wrist clasped in my hand. Tugging her behind me, I grab my credit card from the waitress on the way outside. We reach the car, and the driver opens her door. She gets in obediently, and as soon as I close my door behind me, we sweep into the mass of cars surrounding us. She's quiet, her lips pursued, and her chin held high. This beautiful vixen is tormenting me in ways she has no right to. I lay my hand on her thigh just below the hem of her skirt, and her sharp gaze locks on me.

"What are you doing?" she asks, surprised, but makes no move to stop me or remove my hand. "I didn't agree to anything. Take me home." Her gaze stays glued to my hand, watching what I'm doing. I start with slow strokes up and down her thigh, testing my luck. I want to give her the room to push me away if that's what she really wants.

She doesn't, though.

She simply sits there, watching.

Her legs widen as my hand drifts up a little higher.

"I want to go home," she says again, but this time, her breathing is heavier and her eyes darken and I know for sure that's not what she wants.

Fuck.

CHAPTER 16

Rya

His hand keeps inching higher and higher up my thigh, and I'm helpless to tell him to stop.

Why can't I tell him to stop?

I mean, I should be able to.

I hardly know this man.

Yes, I met him many years ago, but since he's been back in my life, the only thing he and I have in common is that he keeps demanding that I marry him. Which I can't say surprises me, but at the same time, it's totally weird and obnoxious, and the demand is outrageous.

Maybe I should agree to his deal—I have sex with him, and he stops asking me to marry him. I mean, he did stop me from having sex when I really wanted it. So maybe he owes me this one thing. At least that's what I'm telling myself as we sit in the back seat of the car. I'm not even really paying attention to where we're going, just that we're moving, and his hand is still on my thigh.

His free hand, the one that isn't up my skirt, takes my hand and places it on his cock. I can feel his hardness through his trousers. His hand moves higher up my thigh, and my legs spread even wider. I'm pretty sure the car slows, but I'm hardly paying attention right now. He reaches my panties, and I know he can feel my wetness through the lace. He sucks in a breath and gets down in front of me. Luckily for him, this car has a lot of room. He's close, and his eyes are on me as he slides my skirt up ever so slowly. He leans down and places his mouth against my knee, lips lingering for a moment before he kisses up my leg.

"So wet for me, princess." His fingers slide my panties to the side, and I feel him right where I need him.

I should tell him to stop.

That this isn't right.

But it's just sex.

And if we have sex, I can get him to leave me alone.

It's a win-win for me.

At least, that's what I tell myself as his head lowers,

and he pulls my skirt up higher, replacing his fingers with his mouth.

Fuck.

I gasp as his tongue meets my clit, the lace is still pulled to the side, his mouth then moving lower to my entrance.

Tasting me.

He groans, and I lift my hands from my sides to caress his shoulders before I run my fingers through his hair. He needs no direction from me on how to make me feel good. Crue knows what he's doing and how to use his mouth, that's for sure.

His finger slides into me, causing a moan to escape my lips. His tongue continues its slow circular motion around my clit—it's warm and feels fucking fantastic.

My head lolls back against the seat as he pushes in another finger, not slowing his pace with his mouth, and that delicate build begins to wind tighter inside me. I hate how much I fucking love it. How much pleasure he's offering me. And I can't help gently thrusting against him, wanting—no, needing—his tongue deeper. I can feel myself starting to come, and I know he can also feel it.

"Princess, are you going to come for me?"

I have no words. All I can do is reach for Crue's head and put it back where it belongs—between my legs. I grind against his face, and he lets me. He keeps the pace perfect until my hands grip harder, and my body starts to come undone as I let out a small scream. He moves before I have the chance to even catch my breath. I'm still riding that wave of undeniable pleasure even after he's no longer touching me.

I hear a zipper and then the tear of a wrapper. As I finally open my eyes, he pulls me so my legs straddle his lap. The minute my thighs are locked around him, I feel his cock between my legs, and when I look down at him, he looks up.

"Take it if you dare." He says it in a way that makes me want to slap him. As if it's a danger to fuck him.

Does he *not* know who I am?

The shit I have seen and dealt with being a criminal lawyer alone is enough to scar most people.

But that shit has only made me stronger.

So I smile down at him.

"No more offers of marriage," I remind him.

His tongue darts out to lick his lips.

I feel him, ready to nudge inside me, but I press a hand to his chest, halting him. "Tell me you agree." I grip his face between my palms and force his eyes to mine.

"Feisty princess."

"Tell me you agree," I repeat, lowering myself.

Even if Crue doesn't agree, I'm pretty sure I don't have the willpower to pull away. I want this. My body wants this. I want more releases. And to be honest, no man has ever made me come that fast with just his mouth and fingers.

"If that is your demand, princess." He smirks and lifts his hips, pushing himself right inside of me. I freeze, unable to move as I adjust to his size. When I felt him through his pants, I knew he was big... but shit. "Cat got your tongue?" he asks, leaning in and capturing my bottom lip between his teeth. He bites down gently, then pulls back, releasing me with a lick.

"I can take anything you throw at me," I say. I wish it didn't sound so breathless and was more of a match to his cocky tone. *But, fuck, is he big.* He comes back again, this time his lips covering mine as he kisses me, his tongue sliding into my mouth. I can taste myself on him. But I also taste him. This man is like sweet wine and temptation.

I should not be doing this.

I need to stop.

My hips pause, and he pulls back, breaking our lips apart. His hand slides up the back of my leg to my ass, and he squeezes it hard.

"What's the matter, princess?" He thrusts inside of me, and I tense even more. My hands on his shoulders are trying to keep from moving. But he has the upper hand, even if I am the one on top.

"Stop doing that." I smack his shoulder.

"What! This?" And he thrusts again. Before I can open my mouth, he takes hold of my hips and starts to move with purpose, nothing but lust staring back at me in his eyes.

He keeps hitting that magical spot, and my eyes close in pleasure. He fucks me—even though I'm on top and should be in full control—his grip controlling every move. Each moan leaving my lips lets him know how much I want it. How much I'm enjoying every second of this sexual encounter with him.

His hands roam my back and then slap my ass. Hard. He does it again, this time his other hand smacking my other ass cheek before one hand skates up to my neck, then into my hair, twirling it around his fist before he pulls back, exposing my throat. My hands move from his shoulders to grip his knees behind me as I ride him.

Or is he still controlling me?

It's all blending together right now.

And I think he knows he has won this round.

Goddammit! And I hate that he's winning.

I shouldn't want to be anywhere near this man. He is a criminal, and he killed my boss and my date.

And yet I'm letting him fuck me like there is no tomorrow.

But holy heck does it feel good.

My back arches, and his mouth finds my neck. He bites it or sucks it, I'm not sure which, and I'm helpless to stop him anyway. I'm coming, and he tugs my hair a little harder as I do, bending my back more. His cock hits that perfect spot, making me scream.

A lot.

He kisses up my neck until he reaches my mouth and takes control, both hands now gripping my face as his hips pump faster. I feel it when he comes, and we both fall into each other. I ride the bliss until a sharp and painful realization creeps in. Rational thought and lack of discipline sink in my stomach. It only takes me a second to realize why and pull away.

"You can't be disgusted now, princess. Not with how hard you just came." He chuckles.

"I despise you," I say through gritted teeth.

His grip falls free as I climb off him, and even soft, his cock is big. Shit. No wonder he was able to make me scream.

"Show me your tits, and I can fuck you again." He licks his lips as I pull my skirt down.

"Where are we?" I ask.

"At your apartment."

I sigh, relieved. "Good. Bye. Don't call me." I grab the door handle and try to open it, but he reaches for me, and turns my head back to look at him with his hand on my chin.

"No goodbye kiss? No, 'thank you for making me scream'? No, 'no other man has fucked me like that before'?" he asks.

I pause. And smirk.

"No goodbye kiss. And yes, I've been fucked with more passion and more cock before. But I would at least rate you in my top ten."

His grip on my chin loosens, and I take that moment to climb out of the car.

Asshole.

I seem to use that word a lot, but it's so damn descriptive.

CHAPTER 17
Crue

"Top ten," I mutter. "Top ten, my ass."

"What the fuck are you talking about?" Angel asks as she slides on her shoes.

"Angel," Dominic warns, but she merely rolls her eyes before she walks out the door, one of our men going with her. A pang of irritation sparks in me, knowing she's going to see Rya when it should be me instead. But I had to agree to Rya's terms. I can let her think I'm giving up, but I have every intention of making her my wife. She just needs to come to that realization, and the sooner, the better.

"Why are you muttering about a top ten?" Dominic asks, taking a seat next to me. He hands me a stack of paperwork and a pen.

More shit to sign.

It's been a few hours since I dropped Rya off, and she told me I'm in her top ten.

She said it to get under my skin. I know it.

"What's this?" I ask, holding up the forms.

He points to the first one. "The families are asking about your marriage. When it will be done."

"Fuck the families," I grumble.

"This is the extra ownership you get when you marry." He points to a section on the paper that describes extremely lucrative businesses. Ones I have wanted but haven't been able to gain access to yet.

Only when I marry will they be mine.

"Now, why are you grumbling about a top ten?"

I scan the paperwork. There's nothing there that I haven't already memorized. That I know will soon be mine by rights.

I want all of this right now.

The founding families signed this contract. The businesses I've been wanting to manage are now within reach. It's so close I can feel it. And with Rya standing beside me as the most powerful woman—we will be untouchable.

"It's something Rya said," I grit out.

"Do you really think you can get her to agree to

marry you? She hasn't been in our world for a long time."

"But she knows the world, and you know it's always been her." I've been fixated on her from the moment I laid eyes on her. *She's mine.* Contracted or not. The more she fights it, the more I want to break her into submission. To watch the beautiful little vixen admit that she's mine. And mine alone.

"Yes, and I think every other woman you've fucked has known that too." He laughs. "Remember that one time you asked Tiffany to dye her hair and wear contacts when you were fucking her?" He shakes his head. "She was pissed and came out of your room ready to murder someone."

"I have a thing for women with caramel-colored hair," I say, smiling.

"Yeah, I think we all know that." Dominic stands and taps me on the back. "I must say, despite the muttering, you seem less stressed. Did you finally get laid?"

I smile at the vivid memory of Rya straddling me, and it makes my cock twitch.

"Oh shit, you did. Who was the woman?"

"It was her."

His brows raise in surprise. "Well, shit. So are we planning the wedding?"

"She made me promise that in exchange for us fucking, I would stop asking her to marry me."

He smirks at that.

And so do I.

CHAPTER 18

Rya

For two days in a row, I have seen Angel. It's nice to have a visit with her after work and then have some dinner with her. She hasn't brought *him* up, though I know she's dying to.

The first night, she asked me about the mark on my neck. That bastard left his claim on me, and no amount of makeup could cover the dark purple mark entirely. I brushed it off, saying it was some mystery man. But she and I both know that Crue wouldn't let any other man touch me. Which is painfully irritating and sexy as all hell, considering he's visited my dreams every night since.

I shouldn't want it again.

I hate him.

But my body is a treacherous thing.

And it pains me to admit it had been the best sex of my life.

Tonight, Angel sits across from me, glowing with her pregnancy, and I have a feeling she is going to ask. She's mentioned him in passing comments, gauging my reactions. And I've given her nothing.

What is there to tell?

Am I supposed to say, *"Hey, I fucked your brother-in-law, and the sex was amazing. I'm already dreaming about when it can happen again. But did you know he's a psycho and that he kills people who piss him off?"* I mean, she more than likely knows all that already.

We sit in my living room on the couch with the television playing in the background, not that either of us is watching it as we finish our takeout.

She sighs. "I've really enjoyed this. We shouldn't have waited so long to get together again."

I nod in agreement. Life seemed to get so busy so fast. And although it's been fourteen years, having Angel here in my New York apartment doesn't feel strange. It's as if no time has passed between us, and we are back where we were all that time ago.

There's a deliberate pause as she watches me.

"Say it, Angel."

She quirks a smile. She's never been one to be shy

or beat around the bush. Not with me. Not with anyone. And that's saying something, considering she married a man from one of the most established criminal families.

"Do you think you'll ever come back home?"

"To Italy?"

She nods.

"Nope. No interest. This is my home now."

Angel seems a little sad at these words, but she nods as she takes a small bite of her dinner.

"Your name has been circulating a lot back home, you know."

"Because of this marriage shit?"

She nods.

"Has nothing to do with me. I never agreed to it."

Her gaze lands on my neck, and I feel a slight flush of heat across my cheek. A woman has needs. The problem is, I can't entirely deny I wouldn't do it again. There is no way a woman has that much self-control. The man knows how to fuck, and that fact calls to me.

"I have to go back soon, and Dominic is coming with me," she says, reaching for her glass of water. Following her cue, I take a sip of my red wine.

"For the baby?" I ask, gesturing to her belly. She looks down and rubs it, a soft smile on her face. It still seems strange to me when I see her like that. To think that we were teenagers sneaking our parents' liquor and going on an escapade whenever we were given the chance, and now... well, things have changed.

"Yep. We don't want the baby born here. And even if Crue plans to stay here long term, it's not somewhere I want to live."

"Why?" I ask.

"It's too dangerous," she whispers.

"I think anywhere can be dangerous."

She shakes her head and says, "Back home, they know Crue is in charge, but he has to reinstate the name and boundaries here. A lot of the families here have become power-hungry, and Crue's been shedding blood for sport. All to make sure the Monti name is respected and feared."

It goes without saying that movement like that takes a while. A lot longer than being here for only a few weeks.

"How long has he been here?" I ask, placing my glass down.

"Years," she admits.

I don't know why that comes as a shock to me, but it does. Why now, of all times, does he reintroduce himself? Because he has less than a year to fulfill his marriage contract? So why not act on it sooner? Why wait to visit me on my thirtieth birthday and ruin my entire celebration? It was the ultimate dick move.

"He killed my boss," I remind her.

"Yes, I overheard that convo as well." She picks at her chocolate cake with her fork, then pops a bite into her mouth, a bliss-filled smile spreading across her face. Angel always had a sickening appreciation for sweet treats. She points her chocolate-smeared fork at me. "Your boss was dirty, though. And not just that. He also had stuff on you."

"Me?" I ask, surprised. I'd worked with Brian for years. He was ruthless, maybe. But dirty? I doubt that.

"He put cameras in the women's bathroom and kept all the files he had on you. *Just you.* He was nothing but a dirty perv."

I slump back in my seat. "No, he wouldn't have done that," I say, shaking my head. "We would have known."

"Crue is many things, but he's not a liar. And he always has a reason when he kills someone."

"Crue is the type of person to kill someone for looking at him the wrong way."

She shrugs and takes another mouthful of the rich chocolate cake.

"He killed Andrew," I add. "No reason there."

"Yeah, I overheard that one too." She bites her

bottom lip. "Didn't he warn you not to go on a date with him?"

"Yes, but he isn't the boss of me," I say, getting defensive.

"No, he's just the man who killed your boss."

Touché.

A bubble of anger rises inside me. It's not that I'm mad at Angel. It's how calm we are with this conversation. Most likely, it's because we've both seen our fair share of shit and dead bodies. It isn't anything new, and I wasn't attached to Andrew. But, damn. He never deserved that.

"He had no right to walk in and kill Andrew. No matter what he was feeling."

"But in his head, you're his."

His control, which extends even to my best friend, is infuriating. And it's not anyone else's fault but my own for thinking he wouldn't actually kill my date.

"I am not his," I remind her. "I am a person, and I belong to myself."

At this, she smiles a wide smile. "I know that. Why do you think I'm enjoying you giving him a run for his money so much? It's nice to see someone finally put him in his place. He's a little too demanding for my liking." She laughs. "And you're the same, so it's a match made in heaven... or hell." She laughs again.

I can't help but smile as I take another drink of my wine. "You know, this whole situation is fucked-up."

"Don't I know it. But I'm not the one who slept with him." She raises an inquisitive eyebrow.

Before taking another sip of red wine—my personal form of dessert—I easily admit, "I can neither confirm nor deny."

She slips in another forkful of her chocolate cake, her words coming out muffled. "It looks like Crue isn't the only one playing with fire."

CHAPTER 19

Rya

It's been less than two weeks since Brian's murder. And since I haven't accepted the new role, his stuff remains in his office. He didn't really have a family, and not even his ex-wife wanted to collect his things. A testament to how swimmingly their divorce went.

So I came in early, looking for what, I am entirely unsure. But anything that might confirm Angel's claim. I find it hard to believe that Brian was that type of man. We weren't close, but he had given me every opportunity in this firm. And to think he was doing something like that? But what reason would he have? For a personal collection or some kind of blackmail if ever needed, perhaps? I'd been around too long now to know that either was equally possible.

I search his top drawers, disappointed by outdated

documents and a small bottle of unopened whisky. His laptop, phone, and computer screens have all been removed. The police took them when they wanted to investigate further into his murder. With such an easily closed case, they'd returned them, but no one cared to put them back. I mean, he was gone after all.

I pop my hands onto my hips. "Shit," I mumble, feeling half-crazed that I'm looking into this in the first place. I mean, he's dead. But I have to know.

A light tap on the glass door interrupts my rummaging through his drawers. I lift my head to find Mr. Luca looking somewhat confused as he opens the door.

Shit.

"Rya?"

"Good morning," I say with a gentle smile as I continue casually looking through the drawers. If I stop, then I'll definitely look suspicious.

"Good morning. What are you doing in here?" he asks, and I notice the hint of suspicion in his tone.

"I had given Brian a file and was hoping it might be here somewhere. But looks like I'm out of luck." I wave my hand in fake exasperation.

"Don't you back everything up on your computer?"

I nod. "Yeah, I do. I just know he had written notes

down on it, so I was hoping to find it. But I can navigate without it, of course."

There's a long silence.

So, I go below the belt with theatrics. "It's just still so strange that he's gone."

A flash of something cuts across Mr. Luca's blue eyes as if he understands. I'm not particularly affected by Brian's death. I've become desensitized to death over the years. But for the longest time, I was his star pupil. And if I could use that to get out of this situation, then I definitely would.

"It's cut us all very deeply." He looks back at the door and throws a casual finger in its direction. "I could've sworn that door was locked."

I pretend to be confused. "No, I was able to walk in. Maybe the cleaners left it open?" *Actually, I picked the lock.*

A "harrumph" is his reply.

"Why are you here so early?" I ask, suddenly realizing that most of the firm's employees don't clock in for another hour. Mr. Luca has been around a lot more since Brian's death, and I wonder if that's because he's worried one of his biggest investments has a lot of questions revolving around it. Or perhaps his father wants him on the ground doing his dirty work.

"I've just been assisting, you know, with damage control and all."

"Ah." I nod in understanding. "Well, now that I can't find it, I'll go off memory." I walk around the desk and head for the door.

"Is this regarding the Torrisi case?" he asks.

I turn to face him. "No, a different case. Why's that?"

"You're close to closing it, is all. And it seems to be leaning in your favor."

I offer an assured smile. "It always does."

"I just want to make sure you're not having too hard of an issue with them. I know Andreas can be very intimidating. Your meeting the other day looked intense." It takes me a moment to understand what he is referring to. Then it dawns on me. *My meeting with Andreas Torrisi, who asked about Crue.*

"They can all be intimidating. But that's why I'm the best," I remind him. And it goes without saying as to why the board offered me Brian's job. But before he can ask me any more questions, I'm out the door, saying, "Have a good day, Mr. Luca."

Fuck.

And I'm no closer to validating Angel's claims.

CHAPTER 20

Crue

A week without seeing her, tasting her again, is slowly starting to kill me. But I have to put pieces in place, and I need to keep my distance so she thinks she has the upper hand.

She doesn't.

But she's a smart enough woman that she'll figure that out incredibly soon. I never told her how long our agreement would last.

I watch the news, which I never do. But there's a reason I tune in today. Rya's on the channel, being interviewed as she comments on the Torrisi case. It looks like the case will be coming to a close in a few weeks and she's been working on it for the last six months. Even though despite all evidence and the

Torrisi's son recently making a spectacle of himself, she has it under wraps.

She's beautiful, powerful, and unwavering on the screen. She's wearing a knee-length black dress that accentuates all her curves, and her hair is wrapped into a tight bun. I want to tug on that bun and let her caramel hair fall free. To kiss those fuckable lips. I wonder what others might think if they knew how fiery this little vixen is off-screen. My cock twitches. Not that I would ever share what she's like outside of the courtroom. That's for my eyes alone.

She is definitely the only one who can uphold the Monti name and take her place as my wife.

I hear light chatter outside my office. My mother and Angel fluttering about the baby. Since the news of Angel's pregnancy, my mother reminds me daily of my responsibility that it's time I provide an heir.

By my age, my parents had already had Dominic and me. Not that it mattered. They needed an heir out of obligation, but my father never wanted kids. It was obvious in the way he looked down on us and treated us. Dominic saw less of it because my father's attention was mostly on me as the oldest son.

I knew what my father did for work. He'd taken me into many rooms with him where he shot people dead without so much as a warning. He'd even killed a waitress for bringing my mother the wrong type of soup once. No one in the restaurant so much as screamed, let alone went to the body. And we were forced to continue casually dining as blood pooled inches away from my dangling feet. I was five at the time.

How he could do the things he did to make me the best and at the same time try to justify his cruelty, I will never know. I was twelve when I made my first kill. He brought me into a spare room in the house. One I'd studied in multiple times as a child. A man was chained to a seat, hooded, gagged, and bloody.

But that time was different. I could feel the change in the air as my father slapped his sausage fingers on my shoulder and puffed on his cigar.

"IT'S about time you make something of yourself, boy," *he demands as he walks past me and whips the bag off* *the muscled man's head.*

Blood drains from my face.

Curtis.

He's served my family for ten years and was *Dominic's and my personal bodyguard. And now here* *he sits, a half-broken mess. His eyes go wide as my father* *slips a gun into my hand.*

He places his hand on my shoulder again. "Like we've practiced. Shoot him in the head."

"What did he do?" I ask, my voice devoid of any emotion. I knew better then to show a tremble of weakness around my father. Or anyone, for that matter.

"He betrayed us," my father says matter-of-factly. "That's all you need to know. This is an order."

My eyebrows only knit together slightly. I'd seen plenty of people killed. Some of them because they tried to kill me. But this would be the first time I'd be the reason why the life left their body. I saw how it fed my father. In the way that he sometimes took cruel delight in it and in others he was indifferent. That the person was no more than a roadblock in his way to bigger and better things.

How will it make me feel? Will I be the same as him? That's what I was being raised for, right?

"Or do you want your knives?" my father asks, irritated, as if that's the reason for my hesitation.

Curtis is trying to yell something through the gag. I find it strange that such a strong man who had protected us and even showed us kindness was so easily broken.

"I'm going to count to five," my father says.
"One."

I raise the gun and shoot before he even counts to two.

I know the consequence if I don't comply with his demands.

My aim is spot-on and Curtis slumps in his chair, his head hanging as blood oozes down his face.

Without so much as a word, my father leaves the room, taking a small part of me with him. I don't know what part of me it is that he takes, but I know that I feel... nothing. No regret, no pain, no heartfelt goodbye. But no pleasure either. Not like my father. But maybe I'll grow to enjoy being a killer.

IT WAS ONLY a few years later when I turned twenty that I realized the threat I'd become to my father. He'd sharpened me so well that his men began listening to my orders, some even directly disobeying his. And once it was reported to me that he put a hit on me and Dominic with the intention of taking my mother out in the process so he could take another wife and force a much younger heir, I knew it was time to act.

Killing him had been the first time I found any pleasure in taking a life. And I found it almost poetic as I dragged his half-beaten body into that very same room where he'd once forced me to make my first kill. I'd never despised him for introducing me into this world so young. It made me who I was. Strong. Feared.

And that time, instead of the gun, I used the knives, taking into account all the times he'd undermined me. I considered the many times he'd beaten me. The times he'd hit my mother, who took punishment for something miniscule that Dominic or I had done. I'd tried to hide Dominic from it. But he'd had his fair share of kills even then.

But then... it was different.

And it became different the night I tortured my father for fun and shot him between the eyes, taking my official claim as head of the family.

I wonder now, had a woman such as Rya been in our lives how she might've pleaded my case. Not that I cared for what she or anyone thought... but I was curious.

Two weeks have gone by since I've seen or heard from Crue. At first, it had me on edge, but then I slid back into my normal everyday life. I'm lost in my cases, and I made it perfectly clear to Mr. Luca and the board that I won't accept the new role until I've finalized the Torrisi case. A lot of press and money rides on this case, and it's consumed me entirely. Between balancing that and meeting with Angel every spare second, it's understandable I almost forget about Crue, as if that monster had been a figment of my imagination.

Just when I think he's about given up, I look up from my desk and freeze as he lets himself into my office.

"You can't be here," I hiss.

As he closes the door, I look past him at some of my colleagues who are curiously looking this way.

This is bad.

"Princess," he says with an arrogant smile.

"You need to leave." I stand, acutely aware of the onlookers.

He checks around my office, ignoring my agitation. "I haven't heard from you. As your husband, I'm hurt."

"You are *not* my husband," I grit out. When he peeks over my computer screen, I quickly pile up my notes and throw them into my top drawer. Then I cross my arms over my chest and glare at him. "What do you want, Crue? You agreed you would leave me alone."

"I did, and I have. But you ignored my email this morning, and it's an urgent matter."

"Going on a date with you is *not* an urgent matter."

He cracks his neck from side to side. "I wouldn't consider it so much as a date as I would showing off my new prize."

Suddenly, I'm reminded of how much I truly hate this man. "I'm not your prize."

He toys with the few pens in a cup on my desk, and I know he's purposefully doing it to piss me off.

He looks up beneath thick lashes, that arrogant smile widening as he realizes how annoyed I am.

"I'll see you there at nine."

"No."

"Hmm," he all but purrs. "Should I start shooting your colleagues one at a time until you see matters more clearly?"

"You wouldn't." And I feel stupid even saying it. He's proved otherwise numerous times.

His eyebrows rise in challenge. "Or would you be more convinced if I bend you over this desk and fuck you so hard you remember your obedience? Perhaps two weeks was too long to let you roam free."

The thought of Crue having me bent over this desk floods my core, a dull ache left in its wake. And I hate it. I hate it so fucking much how my body responds to him. And his arrogant, cruel smile knows it.

"Is it true about my boss having footage of me?" I ask.

His jaw tics, and his expression darkens. "Angel told you." Not a question. And I almost feel stupid asking him. Except if there's one thing I've learned since meeting Crue again, it's that a bargain can always be struck. He has something I want. And he wants me.

Or so he says. But the way he looks at me, I can't deny it.

"You leave her alone," I warn.

His eyebrows raise again. "You don't give me orders, princess."

"Show me evidence, and I'll come to this 'dick-swinging' party of yours."

"Dick-swinging?"

"Isn't that what it is? To be flashy, to show a Ricci on your arm?"

"Not just any Ricci, a woman who could as quickly put them behind bars as she might be able to get them out. You can see how that might be favorable for some of my... partners."

I rest a hand on the desk and click one nail after the other in consideration. "But if I find out you pull any shit with Angel, I'll put a bullet in you myself."

A dark laugh rumbles through him, and I can see the obvious bulge that swells in his pants. I lick my lips with anticipation at the memory of what it felt like. Of how fulfilling riding his cock could be.

"Okay, princess. Agreed. I'll see you at nine."

A soft knock comes on the door from the only daring soul in this building. We both turn to see Andreas waiting. Colleagues hide behind their desks. Nothing good ever comes of having more than one killer in the room. Especially killers who have gotten away with it for so many years with absolutely no consequences.

"Now, get the fuck out of my office. And don't come back here. I mean it, Crue."

"How I've missed those poisonous lips."

I all but shove him out the door while straightening my black suit jacket.

Crue and Andreas stare at one another. One predator sizing up the other.

This definitely is not good.

"Mr. Monti, I heard you've been in New York for some time. I wasn't so sure. You're incredibly hard to find." And I can feel the edge in his tone, the subtle threat.

Crue's sharp gaze radiates nothing but malice. "I only show myself to those of importance," he replies dryly, then his gaze returns to me. "Be a good girl while I'm gone."

My sharp nails curl into my palms as I watch him leave. I'm unable to say anything because if I do, I'm going to fucking explode in front of all these people.

"Mr. Torrisi, we didn't have a meeting scheduled for today," I say with a tight smile. My attention is still on Crue, who is now flanked by two men. *Where the fuck were they hiding?* Dominic is one of them, and he looks over his shoulder to give me an apologetic grimace.

"We didn't. I just wanted to go over some finer details for the court case since it's coming to an end." He too watches as Crue leaves. "I thought you said you didn't know Mr. Monti."

My sharp gaze meets his. "I'm not at liberty to discuss client matters."

"He doesn't look like a client."

Frustrated, I open my door to let him in. "Of course he is," I say cheerfully. "He's a criminal with a fat bank account. My favorite type of client."

CHAPTER 22

Rya

I'm fuming the entire time I get ready. I'm half tempted to rock up in baggy pants and a hoodie just to seriously piss him off. And yet, I find myself in a tight-fitting red dress and my favorite pair of Louis Vuitton heels. I'm no doubt walking into a den of wolves tonight. More disturbingly, I'll be sitting at the feet of the most dangerous one there.

The driver Crue sent for me pulls in front of what looks like a private restaurant. A bodyguard steps out of the passenger side and opens the door for me, immediately flanking me. I curse under my breath. *He cannot be serious.* This is precisely part of the reason why I left Italy in the first place. I was done with over-protective men in my life.

But I know it isn't the bodyguard's fault. He's just the damn chump taking orders.

When I reach the entrance, he opens the door, and the hostess doesn't bother asking for a name before she directs me where to go. When she pushes open the door, the music hits me first. It's obnoxiously loud. People are everywhere, but it's not overly packed. It's a more upper-class nightclub, kind of like invitation-only style.

"Follow me, Miss Ricci." She winds through a throng of people until we reach a set of stairs. She points up, and I follow her direction with my gaze. I spot Crue straight away, sitting with a few men around him as he leans forward, a cigar hanging from his lips. Acting as if he owns the place. Hell, he probably does. But it doesn't make it any less unnerving as he watches every step I take. Even when I don't look at him, I can feel his eyes burning through me. When I reach him, I chance a glance at him, only to find his dark molten brown eyes drinking me in.

He takes two steps to close the distance between us and leans in, his breath a hot flush against my ear. "You might draw too much attention tonight."

I curve a smile that doesn't reach my eyes. "You do that plenty on your own, asshole."

His devilish smile creeps across his face as he blows smoke from his cigar to the side. "A perfect pair, then."

I take a step back, unable to handle the close proximity of this man. I hate him so much, and yet my body yearns for his next touch. "Show me the evidence."

"Not until you do as you're told," he bites back, then gestures to the men sitting around a table, casually snorting drugs, smoking cigars, and downing whisky.

"So this is her," one of the men says, raising a glass and taking a drink.

Crue takes a seat at the head of the table as a woman comes over and offers me a glass of champagne. I take it, grateful for its bitter taste. It's so fitting for the likes of the men I'm with. Looking back to Crue, I find him still watching me with that cigar between his lips.

To see what?

If I play nice with the others?

"Smoking is disgusting," I tell him, lifting the glass to my lips again.

"Is it?" He takes another puff and rests his elbow on the table. "I wonder what you would taste like if I blew this up you." He blows out another cloud of smoke, which lingers in the air as the lights shine through the haze. My thighs automatically clench together, and it doesn't go unnoticed. It never does.

"Top two, for sure." I wink at him, and he smirks and puts the cigar out, then taps his leg. I will not be sitting on his leg, thank you very much. I sit opposite him and notice his men watching us, but they stay quiet.

"Do you find something funny, Dawson?" Crue asks.

I turn around to find a man standing behind me. He's dressed in a white suit but somehow he pulls it off. You would expect him to look stuck up, kind of a pretty boy even. Except he looks dangerous, not as lethal as Crue, but he has the same energy nonetheless.

"Not at all." He offers a smile that most likely knocks any woman or man off their feet. Then he nods to me, and I can't help but look Dawson up and down. He's perfectly polished, which makes him perhaps one of the most dangerous men sitting in this room. At least with Crue you know he reeks of danger from a mile away. In comparison, Dawson seems more sophisticated.

"Rya." My gaze snaps back to Crue, who is watching me intently. "I'd keep your eyes on me." I offer a sickly-sweet smile as I lift the glass of champagne to my lips. "Dawson, meet my future wife." I choke on my drink, my hand going to my chest.

"It's a pleasure to finally meet you. Crue has told me a lot about you." Dawson takes the empty chair beside me and holds out his hand. I cannot help but simply stare at it.

"What has he told you?"

"That you are an incredible lawyer and have an attitude that rivals his, and let me tell you, that's a hard one to beat." He winks at me, and I look back to Crue, who is smirking.

Well, I'll be damned.

Maybe he does have a friend.

Just the one.

Because had anyone else said that about Crue, he most likely would've shot them.

"I told you to stop with the wife thing," I tell him quietly so only he and Dawson can hear me. Showcase me? Sure, whatever. Tell them I'm your wife? No. I'm done with that. "I think it's time I leave." I stand and make to go, but then Crue's there, his hands sliding around my waist and holding me to him.

He leans down and whispers in my ear, "Princess, we've hardly teased one another enough yet. You want to go straight to fucking instead?"

"You said you'd stop with the wife thing," I reiterate.

"I have. I haven't asked you to marry me."

I hate that he's right. That he finds loopholes in things just like I would in any case I represent. I turn around, and he lets me but keeps his hands on my waist. I can feel the stares of others around us, but he doesn't seem to care. "Let's sit. Drink. Then later..." He backs away and pulls me with him to the seat he occupied. I go to take the seat next to him again, but this time, he tugs me down onto his lap.

Dawson offers me my glass of champagne as if I'm not being restrained against my will. "So you're a lawyer?" he asks.

"Yes, and you are?"

"I dabble in a few businesses. Escorts, mainly." My eyes go wide at his casual admission.

"Escorts?"

He nods his head.

"Dawson here is the top male escort in all of America," Crue says.

"And what do you do for him?" I ask Crue.

"Protection," he replies before he pulls me even closer to him.

Dawson starts talking to someone else, and Crue pulls out a box.

I freeze when I see it.

Another fucking ring box.

"It's not what you think. Just open it." I stare at it, unsure. This could be a trick. I don't really know, and I am not sure I want to take any chances. "Take it. It's not a ring," he tells me.

I do as he says this time and open the box. With shaky hands, I look inside, and sure enough, it is not a ring. And I sigh in relief.

"Don't look so relieved," he says near my ear.

"It's a bracelet?" I say, picking it up. It's too small to be a necklace. I touch the charm and notice it's a C.

"No, it's an anklet. Stand up." He stands too when I'm off his lap, then motions for me to sit back down. He pulls the anklet out of the box and kneels in front of me. He rests my foot on his thigh, then unclasps the chain before he slips it around my ankle and reclasps it.

"Why an anklet?" I ask as he gets back up and sits next to me.

"So when your legs are around my head, you'll be reminded who you belong to."

My mouth opens in shock at his words. "Are you for real?" I ask, outraged.

"Of course I am." He grabs another drink, and before I know it, his mouth is on mine. His hands are on me, and the music fades out as he consumes me.

I hate that he has the power to do that and so easily.

He pulls away just as quickly, then stands and looks down at me.

"This time, I want you in my bed." He offers me his hand. "And I will be your number one."

"Wishful thinking," I say with a sweet smile. My core is flooding with warmth. My body betraying me yet again. "You promised me something for coming tonight."

His cocky smile kicks up as if he's impressed I can remember what I came here for at all. He gestures to a closed door. I open it and step through, realizing it's a small, closed-off private bar. A separate, unoccupied room.

When I turn around, his lips crash against mine. All the promises of before a tease. My body melts into his, my teeth grazing along his bottom lip in hot demand as he pushes me against the door. I feel him growing, the swell in his pants pushing against my stomach.

"You really thought you could walk in here in that, and there would be no consequences?" He trails his lips along my jaw and ear as he grabs my throat, pressing bruising kisses along my soft skin.

"Crue," I manage to groan out. "You promised."

My words barely escape my lips—I am in a world of hurt right now.

He grabs my jaw, forcing our gazes to lock. I hate how my body burns for him whenever he is near me. "When have I ever lied to you? Two fucking weeks I've gone without the feel and taste of that sweet pussy."

The tension coils in my stomach as I notice the black folder sitting on the bar, most likely the evidence he promised. But fuck it. His fingers graze up my thigh, lifting my dress to my hips as he presses himself against my wet heat.

His hand remains forcefully on my jaw. "Say you're mine."

"Fuck off!" I breathe out.

His other hand slips beneath my panties, his fingers making delicate swirls against the already-taut nerves. I all but moan.

His grip tightens on my jaw. "Say it."

My groggy eyes snap back to his, and I blink a few times. How can any man make me feel this good? Those dark brown eyes promise all kinds of wicked things. And who am I to say no? How can I possibly say no? There is no way I can say no!

"Crue." His name leaves my lips as a whimper.

It's his undoing, and his tongue pushes against mine, hard and impatient. My nails rake down his chest in hot demand. I will never say I'm his. But my body, just as demanding, can express things that words never will.

I rip at his belt desperately, that smug smile pressing a kiss beneath my ear. "What's the hurry, princess."

He drops to his knees.

This powerful man kneels before me, licking me through my panties. Tasting me as he rubs the lace against me, causing a delicious friction.

I can't handle it anymore. "Crue, fuck me already."

He chuckles, standing again and rubbing his hard cock when it springs free from his trousers.

"I want you bent over that leather couch. *Now.*" His demand is a command and I am too desperate to defy him.

God, do I want him.

Fuck, do I *need* him.

I do as he says, spreading my legs wide as I bend over the couch. He tears open the condom and slides it over his sizeable cock. When I see it now, hard like this, my mouth waters. He's fucking huge and he is about to impale me.

His gaze roams over my ass and down my tanned legs. He looks like a starved man as he grabs my ass. Hard. It's painful. Dominating. Possessive.

He slips my panties to the side and nudges at my entrance. "What are you willing to do for it, princess?"

"For fuck's sake, Crue."

He thrusts in hard, his name coming out of my mouth like a sudden sweet prayer.

I support myself, holding on for dear life as he drives into me again and again, my body jolting beneath him with every thrust. I shouldn't want this, but God, does it feel good. His chest presses to my back as his hand comes around my throat like a collar. I can hardly breathe as his grip firms, and his thrusts quicken.

Pure bliss rattles through my body as my legs go almost limp. He whispers in my ear, "Do you like that, princess? Do you want me to fill you up?"

"Yes," I whimper. It's all I can do to beg for more. To not let this ever stop.

He turns my head and takes my mouth to swallow my moans and groans, his tongue as forceful as his thrusts while he claims me in every way.

I start to feel lightheaded, wondering if maybe it's too much, and that's when he releases his grip around my throat, his hand trailing down my back until he circles a thumb around my asshole.

He toys with it, his cock hitting that spot inside me over and over again as his thumb slowly enters my ass, stretching me. It's raw and rough and possessive and hot as fucking hell.

My legs begin to tremble as the build-up begins trailing up my thighs.

"Fuck, princess," he pants. "Come for me."

It's not a question but a command.

And as defiant as I am against this man, my body is treacherous in all ways as I explode with his name on my lips. A shudder runs through me. And his cock twitches inside me one more time before he grunts, his power bleeding into me as we pant harshly.

It takes me a few moments to catch my bearings when I feel his arm embrace me, and his hand comes around my throat again. He squeezes as he leans over me. "Two fucking weeks, you drove me crazy, princess." His grip tightens on my ass again, appreciatively, as he pulls out and steps away, doing up his pants.

I run my hand through my hair as I shimmy my dress down.

Am I out of my goddamn mind?

But the moment our gazes lock, I can't regret it. Can't regret this powerful man who knows how to navigate my body like it's his personal mission in life.

"Top two?" he asks with an arrogant smile.

I shrug and flick my hair over my shoulder as I walk

over to the polished wooden bar to pick up the files. "There was no cigar. So, no improvement, really."

I flick open the folder and briefly scan the contents. The first picture is evidence enough of Brian's lies. It's an image of me showering in our women's restroom. Something I frequently do when I go to my hot yoga class before work.

"He deserved a bullet." Crue looms behind me.

I snap the folder shut as I turn toward him. "Maybe, but I don't play at being God."

"You should try it sometime." He tips my chin to meet his gaze. "I think you're scared to try because you know you'll like it."

I offer him a sickly sweet smile. "There are already enough things I like that are bad for me."

"But you do like it. Let me show you what else you might like."

Warmth floods my lower stomach again.

Fuck! If we do this, we'll be lost in each other all night. I shouldn't want this.

He nudges me again, grabbing my attention. "Princess, your mind keeps wandering off."

"I got what I came here for," I say as I push past him.

Surprisingly, he lets me leave the room.

I'm then reminded that ten men were outside the

room the entire time. I hold my head high and nod to Dawson. "It was lovely meeting you."

I don't care about any of them, really, but it makes the situation less awkward as I begin to walk away.

It's not so much that I *have* to look back, but I can sense Crue following me through the crowd. And the same bodyguard from earlier flanks me.

As we reach the cool air outside, I turn on Crue. "Also, I don't like having bodyguards. I can protect myself."

"By kicking your attacker in the balls?"

I smile. "It's effective, isn't it?"

"Crue." Someone says his name, and without thinking, I turn in the direction the voice comes from. I watch in shocked horror as a man raises a gun. He's dressed in holey clothes and looks like he hasn't showered in days. "You deserve this and so much more."

The loud bang echoes through the night. My first thought is that he hit Crue, but Crue's hand touches my back. Don't ask me how I know it's him, I just do. Opening my eyes, I see the man who had the gun is now on the ground, blood pooling around him as he bleeds on the cold concrete.

"I'll take her home." I look up at one of Crue's men—the same bodyguard I'd announced I didn't need only thirty seconds ago. He puts his gun away, in no way affected by killing this man.

"Straight back to her place. Ensure she gets inside and stand at her door until further notice." The man nods his head as if it's an everyday order. Maybe it is for him because he doesn't even seem to blink or care that he just got told what to do.

I turn to face Crue.

I'm so shocked by how quickly everything is happening, and then he reaches for my face. "Goodnight, princess." He leans in and kisses the corner of my mouth before he pulls away and is gone.

"Please, miss, let's get you home," the bodyguard encourages.

What. The actual. Fuck?

CHAPTER 23

Rya

When I get home, I fight with the chain's little clasp around my ankle as if the thing is scorching my skin. My long nails do nothing to help pry it off. When I finally get the damn thing loose, I throw it on top of the black file on my table and head straight for the shower. The bodyguard stands outside my door, and I don't care to invite him in. I still stand by the opinion that I don't need a bodyguard, but what have I gotten myself into?

I struggle with the zipper at the back of my dress, growing more frustrated and impatient. "Fuck!" I yell into the empty room until I can finally unzip the dress. I throw it on the bed alongside my panties and bra. "I have to stop wearing color," I huff out as if that's why all this is happening.

I turn the shower to scorching, then dip under it, relieved by its burn and punishment. I press my hands to the shower wall as I bow my head, the water trailing down my back.

What the fuck is wrong with me?

Crue is bad. Forbidden.

He is chaos. Power.

And the devil himself reincarnated.

But most importantly, he is everything I had purposefully run away from. *He* was the reason why I'd left my old life.

And here I am toying with the notion because of what...

Good sex?

A thrill?

A challenge?

I know none of those things are accurate.

What this is between Crue and me goes beyond the boundaries of those things. Worse than that, it's something I can't put into words because I'm not going to fall for this game.

I *cannot* be with Crue.

And I sure as hell will *not* under any circumstances marry him.

I sigh and twist under the water, my hands close to my chest. The entire bathroom has filled with steam, and part of me wishes I could drown in it.

My thoughts drift back to earlier tonight.

The way Crue feels under my touch.

The way he makes me feel.

The way he fills me.

A low throb thrums through me as one hand drifts down to the spot that demands his touch once more. I curse and retract my wandering hand.

Fuck. Am I out of my goddamn mind?

I turn the faucet and blast jarring cold water all over my body, snapping me to attention. It's exactly what I need.

No, I simply used Crue to get what I wanted, I lie to myself. Although, some of that is partly true.

I wanted proof of those videos. And now I have it. Case closed.

I turn the shower faucet off and twist my white, fluffy towel around me. When I step out of the bathroom, I look at the dress and pick it up, walk straight over to the trash, and throw it in with determination. Definitely only wearing black from now on.

My phone lights up on the coffee table.

Three missed calls from Angel.

Five text messages.

> Angel: Dominic just left with Crue. What the fuck happened?

> Angel: Are you okay?

> Angel: Crue told me you're home and have a bodyguard, but I want to make sure.

> Angel: Rya, call me back I'm stressing out here!

> Angel: Rya, I'm pregnant, and I swear to God if I have to give birth to this baby early, I'm demoting you from godmother.

I pause on that text. She hasn't officially asked me to be the godmother, but the thought brings an odd swirl in my gut—something like responsibly rolls through me.

Oh my God, Rya, get your shit together. *You are not having the child yourself*, I think to myself. But damn did tonight do a number on me.

I FINALLY REPLY TO ANGEL.

> Me: I'm fine. Just need some time to myself tonight. I'll talk to you tomorrow.

A SECOND LATER, her response comes in.

Angel: Promise?

I PUT the phone down and pour myself a glass of red because Lord knows I need it after tonight. It's not the shocking part of having a man killed point-blank in front of me—I'd seen that before—but it's because I keep losing myself under Crue's damn spell. I can't seem to step away from him when I should be bolting for the hills. I came here for a normal life, well, as much as I could, and threw myself into work.

I rub the glass against my bottom lip as I look at the black folder. I've looked at my fair share of damning evidence, but it feels different being on the other side of it. Invasive and infuriating.

I take another sip, put the glass down, collect the file, and sit back on my couch to look through the photographs. Me in the shower. Me doing my hair. Me sitting on the toilet. Eww! *What the actual fuck?*

Was he going to use this against me, or did he just

have some weird fucking kinks? And how long has Crue known about this? Is that why he finally made a move? No, it couldn't be. Could it?

I don't even want to know how Crue found out about this. He is more capable than most of acquiring this kind of dirt. Admittedly, he's probably better at it than me.

I pick up my glass and wander over to the floor-to-ceiling window as I click the tip of my nail against the glass thoughtfully. The life I've built is slowly falling apart, and it only began when Crue walked back into it.

But as I look over my shoulder at the damning evidence against Brian, can I really begrudge him that? But then I also look at the new carpet in my living room where Andrew's murdered body had lain.

No.

Crue is dangerous.

And I should stay away.

But my God, it shouldn't be this hard.

CHAPTER 24
Crue

"I received your calling card," I say to the man chained to a chair in what appears to be an empty warehouse. The reality is that this is a place close to the port that we use regularly to traffic our drugs. Not that this man would live long enough to find out. It took us only four hours to track down where the man had come from, or more specifically, who gave him orders. And in my opinion, that was three hours too fucking long.

Dominic stands against the back wall, throwing glances between me and the man. There's a comfortable electrifying prickle to the air. One that often rises when I'm mad. And I am fucking furious right now.

"Fuck off, Monti." The man spits a line of blood onto the ground. Two of his teeth are already gone.

I smile, step up beside him, and punch him so hard I hear the crunch of bone, and I sure as hell know it isn't any of my bones that have shattered. I catch the edge of his chair, making sure he remains upright instead of keeling over.

The man gasps while blood pours from his mouth. The menacing red substance smears my knuckles from where the skin has broken open over bone.

"I am a reasonable person," I casually say into the cavernous space. My men look at each other, unsure if they should respond. "You tell me what I want to know, and I make your death quick. You don't, and I can make it incredibly, excruciatingly slow. I am happy to oblige either way, so make up your mind." With a quick thrust, I plunge my knife, that's always within reach, into his leg. The man screams and reels as I rip it out, flicking my wrist so his blood splatters on the ground.

"Now, I know the man who came to shoot me tonight might've lost his gig and side hustle because of me reclaiming what was already *my territory*. But I know better than to assume you, or he, had concocted such a plan. And I'm also offended that it was executed so poorly."

"Are you fucking crazy!" He jerks, trying to escape

the exceptional handy work of my men who bound him so neatly.

"I've been called many things," I admit. "But do you know what I am most right now?" I pause for dramatic effect. "Pissed. That's right fucking pissed. Before that little stunt, I was having a swell evening." I grab him by the throat, pure adrenaline coursing through my veins. "Give me the name of the person who sent out the hit."

The man chokes, gasps, and squeaks. Pathetic!

I release my grip on his throat, edging my ear closer. "I didn't hear you."

"To—" He coughs. "The Torrisi family did."

I should have fucking known.

"See, that wasn't so hard." I turn my back on him, then pull my gun out of my trousers and spin back toward him, my arm pointed in his direction.

Bang!

The pacifying sound silences his final plea.

"Clean this up. I want as much as you can gather on the Torrisi family and who's in charge now." I stride to the door, and Dominic follows me. I should've known that Andreas would be a fucking problem. And it only complicates things that Rya is working on his nephew's case. Not that I give a shit, but it means there's a small chance she might be targeted because of our association.

"Crue, are you sure you want to act on this so quickly?"

I spin on him, confused and almost certain I couldn't have heard him correctly. "What?" I hiss.

"You might want to let the blood dry before hacking at more heads."

I shove him against the wall, my blade to his throat. "She was fucking there, Dominic."

His hands are raised in defense, and his eyes are wide. "I'm not the enemy," he reminds me. I stare at him, so fucking furious that I want to burn the world down and everyone in it.

Hesitantly, Dominic adds, "This is the world you are asking her to come back to."

"Then I'll cut down every founding father in New York if I have to ensure she's safe." I release him, pocketing my knife and smoothing back my hair.

"Why are you going this far for her? This is... *unlike you*."

"Because she is my soon-to-be wife. I will not show weakness, not even through her."

Dominic considers his words carefully before he says, "I think you already have, brother."

I stare him down. Wanting to tear out his jugular with my bare hands.

He raises his hands in the air again. "I will find out what I can," he says quietly before walking away.

And I'm left alone in the dark, wanting to murder half of New York in payback for ruining Rya's and my night.

CHAPTER 25

Rya

M y face curls up in a cringe at the piles of baby clothes and toys surrounding me. It's not that I have anything against babies or children personally, but I'm not a person who has an interest in being in a store like this.

"What about this one?" Angel asks, raising a pink dress.

"I think they should cap your credit card at some point." Because for a pregnant woman complaining about how sore her feet are, she should not be able to shop up a storm like this. Or at least I wish that were the case to put me out of my suffering.

"Ha. Ha. Very funny. But you're right. Maybe I should go with the more vibrant one over there." She puts it back and waddles across the room while I sigh, drowning in my own personal hell.

"So, remind me again why Dominic isn't doing this with you."

She rolls her eyes, though I can tell she enjoys the company. "They're busy this week with work."

This time, I roll my eyes at the term "work." "And what little side business is experiencing their wrath this week?" I joke.

She puts down the dress and looks at me. "Rya, what happened the other night was pretty serious. I don't know how you're so chill about all of it." She glances at her bodyguard as if he might report back our casual conversation.

I'm grateful enough that I sent only one message to Crue two nights ago, informing him that if he doesn't remove the bodyguard, I'll never have sex with him again. Not that I exactly intend to follow through on that threat, but it seemed pretty effective.

"I know that. But c'mon, we've seen our fair share of shit. And stuff like this happens in New York all the time. Granted, Crue is a larger target than most, for obvious reasons, but life goes on."

Angel wearily side-eyes me. "I think he's doing this for you."

"For me?" I choke out. "The only thing Crue wants to do for me is throw a bun in the oven and lock me up in a castle to bake it so he can fulfill his contract. No, thank you."

"I'm worried, Rya. He's not going to take no for an answer."

"It's just sex. I made that *very* clear."

Her eyes widen. "I knew it!" She smacks me on the arm.

"Ow." I rub the sore spot. "It was only once. Well, actually, twice."

"Rya!"

"What?" I laugh. "Am I half out of my mind for fucking Crue Monti? Yes. Is the sex fantastic? Unfortunately, that's also yes."

She laughs. "It's strange you don't ever really talk to me about this stuff," she admits.

"Why would I? Men come and go like the seasons."

She gives me an even stare. "I don't think Crue intends to be a season, Rya."

"He is until hell freezes over."

"Be careful what you wish for. It might have already." And as quickly as the words leave her lips, her eyes grow large, and she coos, "Ooh, this one is cute."

I sigh. But the warning in Angel's tone is enough to leave me slightly unnerved.

Crue will never be more than a season.

Even if he put a gun to my head.

CHAPTER 26

Rya

Since the night Crue gave it to me, I haven't worn the anklet, and I'm not sure I ever will again. Actually, I'm unsure if I want to see him again. The sex is great, but is that enough to let a killer come back to your bed? No matter how perfectly I build my case that I need to rid Crue from my life, I'm equally as exasperated and fantasize about when I might next taste him and have his body against mine for a brutal, harsh fuck.

I've received many emails from Crue this week and haven't replied to any of them. But that doesn't seem to bother him at all because he keeps sending them, and in snippets, he'll tell me about his day and what he plans to do to me. To be honest, every day when I arrive home, I expect to see him at my door, and a part of me is relieved when he isn't there, while the other part is wondering why he hasn't even tried.

This is Crue, after all.

And his stalker level is the real deal.

Miss Ricci

I hope you are deleting these emails once you've read them. And let's be honest, I know you're reading them. Just as I know, you are more than likely pursing your lips at me right now as you read this.

I'm writing to tell you that I plan to have you for every main meal, including dessert. Did you like it when my tongue slid between your legs while I tasted what was made for me?

Now, remember, don't lie.

You may be wondering where I am this week, as my earlier emails told you I was working.

I'm due back tomorrow.

Be waiting, princess.

Reply this time.

Crue

I GOT THAT EMAIL YESTERDAY.

And today, when I arrived home, I fully expected to see him waiting for me at the door. But, like the rest of the week, he hasn't shown up.

I open the door and lock it straight away, even though that doesn't do anything to stop him. My phone dings, alerting me to another email.

Miss Ricci
I suggest you remove all your clothes, leave your bag in the living room, and come to your bedroom naked. You have five minutes before I punish you.
Crue.

FIVE MINUTES before he punishes me? What does that even mean? Punish me how?

"You better not be in my *fucking bedroom*!" I yell. "That's taking your stalking to the next level."

I hear him chuckle.

And get my answer.

"Four minutes," he calls out.

Four minutes until what? I put my bag down and grip my phone in my hand. I am *not* getting naked and walking into my bedroom. He's fucking dreaming if he thinks that. I wonder if I should grab some type of weapon, but I have a feeling that this man would never hurt me. I contemplate for a few moments if I should walk in there and kick his ass out instead.

I sit on the couch and turn the television on. That man is not the boss of me, that's for sure. I watch the clock tick down because I know he'll come find me once it hits five minutes. I don't know a hell of a lot about this man, but I do know that with everything in me, he means what he says when it comes to me.

Three minutes.

I watch the screen, not taking anything in.

Two minutes.

My hands are sweating.

One minute.

I count down in my head, and when I reach five

seconds, I feel hands slide around my throat and know it's him.

He applies pressure, and his breath tickles my ear. "You want to disobey me, princess?" he asks in a low voice laced with mischief.

"You aren't my boss," I remind him.

"Aren't I?"

"No." I try to turn my head to the side to look at him. "Now, remove your hand." It's then I realize the man is not wearing a shirt. He releases me and steps around the couch. My gaze locks on him, and I'm surprised to find he's naked. It doesn't seem to bother him in the slightest that my eyes scan him from head to toe. I literally can't help it. He's tanned and toned. He has a bit of ink laced on his torso. He has no shame whatsoever when he stops directly in front of me, blocking the television. And he's watching me intently.

"I missed you," he says.

"I didn't miss you." I smile, but it's more sarcastic than happy.

"Are you sure? Every email I sent was opened within two minutes of receiving them."

"Why are you tracking that?" I ask, my gaze dropping to his cock as it bounces. It's hard. And thick. And long. I look him up and down and grin when I reach his eyes.

"I track things I like." He bends so his face is level with mine. "Have you missed me?"

"No," I answer outright.

"Now that's a lie. Let's make a rule not to lie to one another." His fingers touch my chin and lift it so we are eye-to-eye. When he's happy with the position, he moves his hand so it slides ever so slowly down my neck. But he doesn't stop there. With one hand, he begins to unbutton my shirt. My hands stay at my sides, unable to move or stop him as he holds eye contact with me. "One day, I *will* be calling you my wife," he tells me.

"You *think* you will be," I reply. "Or did you forget our deal?"

"I haven't asked you again, have I?" Crue says, and before I know it, my shirt is completely undone. And when I look down, I watch him heading for my skirt. He uses both hands and easily pulls it off, lifting me to do so. Before I can say anything, he throws me over his shoulder and slaps my ass. Hard. I have a G-string on, so when he rubs my ass where he just smacked it, I feel it.

He enters my room and places me in the center of the bed. When I go to get up, I feel something wrap around my ankle. Then he moves to my hand, lifting and kissing the palm before he ties that too. When he grabs my other hand, I pull it away.

"What are you doing?" I ask.

He reaches for my hand again, but he's gentle as he secures it before he goes to my other leg.

"Bondage? Really?"

He steps away from the bed to pick up something from the floor. When he turns back to me, there is a knife in his hand.

"You do *not* get to touch me with that," I warn, pulling on the restraints. Crue doesn't say anything as he approaches, then stops at the end of the bed with his knife in hand.

I see a glimmer of something in his eyes. An almost playful smirk touches his lips as his gaze roams me up and down.

"Crue," I warn.

He locks eyes with me. "Say my name again."

"Asshole!" I yell and pull against the restraints.

"When I make you come, you better scream my name. Remember it on those lips when you do." He leans down, lifts the fabric of my G-string at my hip, then cuts it with the knife.

"That was a very expensive piece of lingerie," I tell him.

"I'll buy you more," he says before he moves to the

side of the bed, where he proceeds to cut my already unbuttoned shirt away from me, leaving me in just my bra. "One piece left." He touches my stomach with the hand holding the knife. He drags his fingers up, the knife sliding along my skin. It feels both hot and cold —hot from his fingers and cold from the knife. Before he gets to my breasts, he lifts my bra and slides the knife under the material, cutting it away as well.

"I liked that bra."

"I'll buy you the entire store," he says, dropping the knife. He again moves to the end of the bed, looking down at me. His hand wraps around his cock, and I can't look away as he slides his hand up and down the massive cock. "Now, remember, no lies." I watch him, fascinated. "Did you miss me?"

"No," I say immediately.

Crue releases his cock and slaps me hard on my clit. He smirks and pulls his hand back. "Maybe I didn't ask the right question." His arms hang at his sides now, and my pussy tingles from the spanking it just received. "Has your pussy, missed me?" I go to open my mouth when he holds up a finger.

"Lie, and you'll be punished. Tell me the truth, and I'll reward you."

"No," I tell him again, pulling against the restraints.

He turns and walks out the door. I struggle to try to free myself, but it doesn't work. Crue comes back with the anklet I haven't touched since I forcefully removed it the night he gave it to me. *I really am out of my fucking mind for wanting this, aren't I?* He bends down to clasp the anklet back on, the dangling letter C cool against the skin of my ankle. Content with his gift once again gracing my body, he leans down and blows lightly between my legs before he slaps my clit again. Even though I pretend to hate it, my hips thrust up against my will, and he notices.

"Stop it," I demand.

"Do you really want me to stop? The last time I was inside you, you quite enjoyed it." This time, he lowers his mouth to taste me, spreading my pussy lips with his tongue.

I moan.

Shit.

"It's not normal to hold someone against their will. Actually, it's illegal," I inform him.

He chuckles. "Lucky for you, I love to dabble in crimes." He leans back down and licks me again.

Fuck me, why does his tongue have to feel so good down there? My ass lifts off the bed, and he does it again and again. Until his mouth pulls away, and I lift my hips, hoping to find him. When I open my eyes, he's watching me.

"You *will* keep your eyes open," he orders. I nod because now I've come to that part where I want to be a good girl and get what he's promising me. "Top ten, huh?" he says, coming around the bed until he's near my head. "Why do I feel like that's a lie?" He fists his cock, leans forward, and rubs the tip against my lips. I lick it, my tongue darting around in circles. "See, princess, you're such a good girl. I didn't even have to ask you to do that."

Crue sweeps an appreciative look down my body as I tug against the restraints. But I'm fixated on the way he strokes himself. How the muscles bulge in his arms, and he stands over me expectantly. It's a slow, beautiful torture. "You're so beautiful when restrained."

He pulls back and continues sliding his hand up and down his cock before he thrusts his hips forward and comes all over my stomach. I look down, and my pussy clenches with need.

How can this be healthy?

How can I want this?

I have no answer except I sure as shit do.

And I want to slap myself for even thinking that, but my hands are tied. So that's impossible.

And as he returns to the end of the bed, the doorbell rings.

We both freeze for a moment, and a key turning in the lock is heard.

His hard gaze finds mine. "Who has keys?" he asks harshly.

"What?"

"I suggest you tell me if you're seeing another man. I'd hate to make a mess on your floor again." I watch as he reaches for something on the floor, and when he stands, he's holding a gun.

He smirks and walks out.

Naked.

Leaving me tied to the bed.

CHAPTER 27
Crue

From what I've gathered, she hasn't been in contact with another man—other than the one I killed—so if she thinks she can get another man by me? Yeah, that's not happening!

"You are a walking red flag, you know that, right?" she yells.

"Luckily for you, red is your favorite color besides black," I yell back. I know this for a fact. She always wears red lingerie, and I fucking love it.

"Rya?"

I stop at the sound of the voice. That doesn't sound like a man. I move the gun in front of my cock to try to hide it as I hear footsteps approaching. I back up when she comes into view. I know who it is immediately—she looks so much like Rya but just a bit older. Except something is missing in her eyes when she looks at me. And I know that look. It's the look of someone who is dead on the inside, devoid of emotion.

Then her eyes go wide and scan me before a smirk forms on her lips.

"Well, I didn't expect to see this," she says.

"Mother, avert your eyes," Rya yells from the bedroom.

I keep slowly backing up.

"You gave me a set of keys. Told me to come whenever I could. I told you last week I would pop by. You work crazy hours, and nights are my only chance to see you." I hear Rya groan from the bedroom. All the while, her mother continues to stare. "And who are you?"

"He's nobody," Rya calls out.

I hold out my hand—the one that isn't holding my gun that's covering my junk.

"Crue, your daughter's future husband."

She glances at my hand and takes it.

"He is *not*!" Rya loudly disagrees.

"Should I send your mother in to talk to you, princess?"

"No. *You* get in here *now*. Mom, wait in the kitchen, please. I won't be long."

"If you say so, dear." Her mother turns and walks

away. When she gets to the hallway that leads to the kitchen, she looks over her shoulder and grins. I smile back and wait until she's gone before I hurry back to the bedroom. I find Rya still tied to the bed, my cum having dripped down her stomach and onto the bed.

And...

... she is furious.

"How dare you! Untie me," she growls as I shut the door. I step up to the bed between her spread legs, bend down, and slide my tongue between her pussy lips, tasting her one last time. Because now she is pissed, she may throw me out. But I came here for her, And I sure as shit plan to leave with the taste of her on my lips at least.

"Stop it! Oh my God..." The first two words are said in anger, but the last three? Well, they just edge me on to keep going. I do it again, tasting her before I slip in a finger, feeling her tight channel immediately tighten around my finger.

"Princess."

"Hmm." She has completely forgotten her mother is here, but I haven't. I stop just as her back arches and pull away. Her eyes fly open, and she glares at me.

"Time to dazzle the new in-law." I wink at Rya, then undo the restraints slowly. I feel her stare on me as I take my time. It penetrates me.

She's mad.

And I can't hide my smile.

"You think this is funny?" she asks as I reach for her wrist. When it's free, I move around to do the other one. She pulls both her hands to her chest and sits up. I catch sight of the anklet, and my cock hardens.

I plan to have that ankle over my shoulder at some point, so when her feet are in the air, she'll never forget who she belongs to. *Me.*

Rya stands and stretches her neck from side to side before she steps closer. Her eyes, which are usually silver, darken, and she drops to her knees, her hands gripping my waist as she digs her nails into my skin. Her lips wrap around the head of my cock, and she takes me into her mouth.

Fuck, that feels good.

I grab her hair, and she swats my hand away, but she stays where she is, her head bobbing up and down, up and down, taking me deep. I tip my head back and close my eyes as a groan leaves me at the overwhelming feeling. At the sound, she pulls away. When I open my eyes, I find her standing, wiping her lips with the back of her hand before she walks to her closet. She grabs a maxi dress, slips it on, and grins mischievously as she walks out the door.

"Finish yourself off. Because when you leave, I am going to do exactly that for myself."

Like hell, she will.

CHAPTER 28

Rya

My mother smiles when she sees me. She stands from her place on a stool at the counter and opens her arms to gather me into a hug. I've always felt awkward hugging my own mother. I never really understood why until recently. It feels incredibly forced like she does it because she thinks I want it. I'm unsure where she got that idea from, but I never turn her down. I won't push her away, either.

We are two very different women. The only thing we are similar in is how calculating we are. If there is one thing in this life that my mother is good at, it is manipulating people to do exactly what she wants. In contrast, I am an expert at manipulating the truth in a courtroom to get others to believe that my clients are innocent. I never really put it together until I saw her in action at work one day. She was complaining about the cost of an item but then proceeded to sell it to someone else as if she hadn't spent ten minutes badmouthing it and telling me it absolutely was *not* worth the price. However, when a client walked in front of her, her mask was on, and she had that item sold within five minutes.

"That was quite an entrance," she says bluntly. I didn't really think she would sugarcoat it anyway.

My mother lives alone, so she has the opportunity to see multiple men. Her apartment is expensive and lavishly decorated, and I always wondered where she got the money to pay for it. The thing about my mother is she has a taste for rich men. And it's served her well.

What she never wanted was a child. But when she was with my father, it was all he ever wanted. So, in exchange for a healthy prenup when they got married, if she could supply him with a child, in the terms of the divorce, my father would keep the child, and she would be paid thousands of dollars every month. I only discovered this later in life. If I knew this when I was sixteen and chose to live with her, I probably would never have done it. Funny how little truths like that can make a difference.

"Are you two an item?" Mother asks.

I pull away and go to the refrigerator to grab a juice, replying, "No."

"Yes," comes from the other side of the room. Crue walks in, fully dressed, and passes my mother to stand beside me. "I'll be back. I have some work to take care of." He leans down to kiss me, and I pull away. He merely smirks before he kisses my forehead. "I'll bring dinner."

"Don't come back," I call after him. "I paid him for sex, and he thinks he can come and go as he pleases. Really, these prostitutes have no clue," I say, making him pause on his way to the door.

He turns slightly to look over his shoulder at me. "I'll expect payment later." His words are sharp, and I can't tell if he's pissed or amused. He nods to my mother, and then he's gone. I hear the door shut and then lock, and immediately I want to know how that man got a key to my apartment in the first place.

I look up to find my mother studying me. She stares at me with amusement before grabbing and checking her phone.

"Is he one of your father's men?" she asks.

"No." I shake my head. "Why would you say that?"

"Because he has the same energy. What do you kids call it these days? Oh yes, that's right, big dick energy.

Well, that saying is true physically and mentally." She waves her hand in front of her face.

"Oh my God, you did not just refer to his penis."

"Please, kid, your mother gets more penis than you do."

"So, not something I want to know about."

She smirks, putting her phone back down.

"I ask because I want you to know *that world* is dangerous."

"Do you care?" I ask. "I mean no disrespect... but you left me in that world, and I know it better than you do."

She nods in agreement. "I guess you're right. Those men, though... those men who are used to so much power, tire of us women quickly and move on to the next best thing. You aren't like that. You have never settled down because you don't settle. But I believe when you finally do, it will be because you will have put your all into it."

"Are you okay?" I ask, concerned. She never talks to me like this. It's always surface stuff, things that don't matter to her.

"Yes, of course. I know I suck at this parenting thing. It's why I agreed to the deal with your father. He was a great father, was he not?"

"He *is* a great father," I correct her.

"Yes, of course." She chews on her bottom lip. "I never wanted kids, but I wanted power and money." *I already know this.* "So when you came to live with me, I had to get used to that... to you. And despite my shortcomings, you were a remarkable child and now are a remarkable adult. I'm not proud of a lot in this life, but you... well, shit. You are one of the best lawyers there is, and I am so very proud of you."

I smile at her, waiting for the backhanded compliment or a request.

But it never comes.

"Thanks, Mom. That's the nicest thing you've ever said to me."

"There is a point." She holds up a finger. "Just because that man has a great cock and can probably use it, don't fall into his trap. You are in control. Remember that."

"Got it!" I nod my head.

"Good. Now, tell me everything because it's been a long time since a man has looked at me the way he looks at you." I blush and wonder if it's just a phase for him too.

Because for me, he's just another season.

IT'S LATE when the door opens. I'm curled up on the couch, watching Netflix, and half asleep. I don't have work tomorrow, so I tend to dull my brain and turn it off. And the way I do that is by bingeing something on the television.

I immediately catch the scent of food, and it smells amazing. I look at Crue entering the room with a bag in his hand. He saunters to the coffee table, places the food down, and then pulls the table closer to the couch before sitting next to me.

"You can't keep letting yourself into my place," I tell him.

"I can and I will," he states. Then he turns to me. "Are you planning to have more visitors?"

"No, but if I did—"

"I'll deadbolt the door the next time I tie you to the bed," he says casually as he takes the food out of the bag.

"What's this? And who said there will be a next time?"

"My mother made it for you." He pulls out two containers.

"Your mother?" I ask incredulously.

"Yes. She's here in New York and will return to Italy with Angel and Dominic." He pauses. "And she wants to meet you."

"I don't want to meet your mother." I scoff.

"Why not?" he asks, handing me a container full of pasta. "No meat," he adds.

I look him in the eye and say, "Because we are people who like to fuck. There is nothing more to it."

"If you say so." He winks and digs into his own pasta. I grab the fork he stuck into mine and take a bite. It's really good. "She's an amazing cook," Crue says.

"She is," I agree. It makes me miss home, just a little. I haven't been back since I was a teenager because my life has been too busy. But I plan to go back. Hopefully, one day soon. "Why are you really here?" I ask.

"Because you are." His answer is simple and seems genuine. I focus on the television, but I don't even know what's happening anymore because he's implanted in my brain. And he's stuck—he won't leave, literally and figuratively.

I eat the bowl of pasta, and when I'm done, he takes it from me, places it on the coffee table, kicks off his shoes, pulls my legs over his, and then covers us with the blanket. He laughs at something on the television, and I stare at the fine lines around his mouth. He really is a perfectly made human. If I had met him as a normal person—you know, without him killing my boss and all—and he asked me out on a date, I would have thought he was talking to someone else. That's how goddammed handsome he is. But not handsome in a clean, pretty-boy way. I can see the rough hands. I have felt them when he touches me. He has these lips that you just want to kiss and never stop. I honestly think I could never tire of kissing this man.

All of that does not equate to me wanting to marry him, though. Nor does it make me want to fall in love with him. Maybe in another life, we could be together. But we want different things. We have entirely different lives.

I scoot down lower, and he kneads my feet while he watches the television. The feeling is overwhelmingly good, and my tired body gives in.

And before I know it, I fall asleep.

CHAPTER 29
Crue

When I carried her to the bedroom, she didn't even open her eyes. I laid her down and pulled that maxi dress off without hesitation. When I did that, she moved but only slightly. Then I pulled the blanket up to cover her stunning body and went to the bathroom. When I came back, she was passed out again.

I kissed her forehead and told her I'd be back.

And right now, it's six a.m., and I'm still not back.

Instead, I stand over a man who looks like he used too much gel in his over-slicked hair as he smiles up at me with gold teeth.

Are gold teeth still a thing? Surely not, it looks so damn crass and unrefined these days.

"Her mother hired an investigator today," he says.

Slimy Jim is his name, and he may be a slimy bastard, but he is good at finding information. He shovels more food into his mouth and mumbles, "She moves fast."

"Who was the investigator?" I ask.

He laughs, then gives me a shit-eating grin, food stuck in his gold teeth. "Me."

I roll my eyes. Of course, it was him.

"And?"

"Well, she wants me to dig up dirt on you."

"Is this at her request? Or her daughter's?"

"She wouldn't say." He shrugs.

Interesting but not surprising. Rya's mother dabbled in this world for a while, and information was of value. Or maybe she genuinely cares about her daughter. But somehow, I doubt that—I know what this woman is like. Maybe it's that she doesn't understand the magnitude of who I really am.

"Then give her some dirt. I want to see what she does with it."

His spoon pauses, and he looks up at me. "Are you for real?"

I clench my hands. Usually, when someone comes poking into my personal business, I kill them. Nothing good comes from someone snooping where they shouldn't be snooping, and the easy fix is to kill them, just as I'd been doing the past week with the Torrisi in mind.

"Yes, but nothing she can use. Make shit up for all I care. Keep me informed, though. I want to know *exactly* what you tell her."

"You plan to let her breathe?"

"Fucking hell, Jim, stop asking questions and just fucking do it." I walk out of his restaurant and slam the door as I leave. Dominic is waiting for me when I slide into the car in a foul mood.

"What's that about?" he asks, dropping his cigarette to the ground before stomping on it.

"The mother may be an issue."

"I don't think Rya will take kindly to you killing her mother."

"Maybe."

"She won't," Dominic says and gets in the car.

Well, damn, there goes that idea.

CHAPTER 30

Crue

I sit across from the collector.

More accurately, the both of them. The sister, Anya Ivanov, sits at her wooden desk. A few guards behind her watch us warily. She has rich porcelain skin with thick, glossy red hair. Her brother, Aleksandr, is posted at her right, watching intently, his red hair the same shade as Anya's. Both look ageless, but I assume they are more or less around my age. Equal partners with different roles to play. Another family dynasty.

Dominic and Dawson stand behind me. My other two men were made to stand outside.

"I'm surprised to see you here today, Mr. Monti," Anya says. "If my intel is correct, you've been living in New York for quite a few years now but have never shown interest in... our events. Why now?" Her smile is polite, but her eyes betray her as her gaze roams over my body. *Desire.*

"I will soon be coming into an inheritance, one might say. And I want to expand my reach and businesses here in New York."

She side-eyes her brother. "I'm sure you're aware that we have many powerful families who attend such events and auctions. I would hope that your intent is pure."

I try not to scoff. *Pure?* That's ironic, considering the business they run.

"Are you saying I don't belong amongst these powerful families?" I question.

She kicks up a smile. "On the contrary. I just hope you don't scare any of my patrons away."

"You can understand why we might be hesitant in your sudden interest," Aleksandr finally speaks. And his voice is as honeyed as his sister's. Two individuals who are equally able to get their own way.

With most.

But I grow impatient, and the atmosphere in the room changes.

"Of course, we are more than happy to accept your entry," Anya quickly says. "But new members often offer a donation of sorts."

"A donation?"

She waves her hand. "Two million is the standard. But I imagine you are not the ordinary." This time she leans forward, nothing but malice in her gaze. "And perhaps... dinner."

Her brother scoffs. "When was the last time you actually dined with a man?"

"There are different types of delicacies." She looks me up and down, biting her bottom lip.

"I'm married." I shut her down.

I probably would have taken her up on her offer a few weeks ago because why not? She is, by definition, beautiful and poised. But she is *not* Rya.

She lifts a brow at my empty ring finger but says nothing about it. "And what will you be offering at the first auction? Aside from your generous donation," she asks with another smile.

Dawson clears his throat. "That would be me."

"Well, well, well..." She leans back with an appreciative glance. "Mr. Dawson in the flesh. What could you possibly get from being on auction when you can already fetch such a high price for your services?"

He shrugs casually. "A change of scenery, perhaps. It is, after all, foreplay, isn't it?"

Anya's mischievous smile widens. "I must confess, I'm exquisitely happy to have you join us this Friday night at midnight."

She offers a sleek black card with only an address. "Welcome to the Ivanov Auctions."

Dominic leans over and takes the card, pocketing it.

Not long later, we leave the luxurious hotel, and I look at my phone.

No reply from Rya.

Dammit!

No surprise there.

And yet, her stubbornness brings a tight smile to my lips. The little vixen.

"Perhaps I should be asking for a generous donation as well," Dawson says, standing beside me.

"Maybe your rates are too cheap, and you should learn to ask for more."

He chuckles at that.

"Are you sure about this? Once it's done, there's no going back," Dominic warily adds.

My jaw tics, and I glare at him. Since coming to New York, he's questioned my methods multiple times. He doesn't understand what it takes to clean these houses, and this is nothing more than another cleanse. Granted, they made it personal when Rya was put in danger.

He grows silent and nods, opening the car door for me.

Everything is beginning to roll, and next will be the new head of the Torrisi family.

He's standing out front of my work, leaning against his car, waiting for me. He's been sending me more emails, telling me about his day. I thought my lack of response might offer a hint, but Mr. Monti played within his own insufferable league.

Dear Miss Ricci
I am most apologetic about the sweet little
red pieces I cut.
Let me make it up to you.
Reply.
Crue

Dear Miss Ricci
I will quite enjoy when you sit on my
face and let me eat you out, wifey.
Reply.
Crue

Dear Miss Ricci
It is not in your favor that you don't
reply to my emails and requests.
Or maybe you like being tied up and
treated like a very bad girl.
Reply.
Crue

I CAN'T HELP but smile at some of these email messages, and the thoughts of what he promises are absolutely tempting. It wasn't until one of my work colleagues pointed out that I was smiling that I realized I was doing it. Now that I'm conscious of the fact I am doing this, I am hyperaware and try my hardest not to give them any response.

Even though I open them immediately after I receive them. I simply can't help it.

"Looking absolutely delicious as usual, princess." He reaches for me and pulls me into him. "I see you've been reading my emails all week."

My hands rest on his chest as I look up at him. "You send one every day, sometimes twice. And I thought I told you to stop coming to my work."

"I contemplated sending one every time you crossed my mind but figured that was too many, and you may not be impressed with that." He winks and possessively grabs my jaw, adding, "And you don't give me orders." Before I can reply, he leans down and kisses me. It's soft at first, then his hand slides to the back of my head, and he becomes more demanding. His other hand pushes my ass even closer to him, closing any space there was between us.

"Bye, Rya," one of my colleagues says as she walks past.

Shit. People are becoming accustomed to him being around.

I pull back and offer a wave without looking.

His thumb swipes at the bottom of my lip. "You have lipstick everywhere," he says.

"That's because you molested me," I grumble.

He smirks, then pulls back and opens the car door. He motions for me to get in.

"I have plans for us tonight," he tells me as I climb in.

"Plans? Maybe I have my own plans."

"What did we say about lying? Would you like me to punish you now?" His face is close to mine, his dark gaze penetrating. He waits for me to answer, but I simply grin. When I say nothing in return, he shuts the door, walks around to his side, and slides in next to me.

"What are the plans?" I ask.

"Well, tonight, we'll be at my place. But first, I have to take you somewhere."

"Where?"

"I seem to owe you a lot of red lacey things."

"Two, to be precise," I remind him.

"Yes, two." He nods. And that's all the answer he gives me. Through the window, I take in the busy New York evening in comfortable silence before we come to a stop.

"Where are we?"

"My building," he says and offers me his hand.

I take it and follow him out of the car. I spot a familiar face as soon as we walk into the building. Dawson is standing there and offers me a gentlemanly smile. He always seems so polished. Crue keeps his hand on my lower back as he leads me into a bar area. It's quiet, but I notice a bunch of women in the corner who are wearing robes.

"Red, you requested?" Dawson asks, and I look at him, confused.

"Yes, Dawson, red."

"Easy." He nods and moves over to the women in the corner.

"What is Dawson doing here?"

"Dawson owns multiple lingerie chains. He's flown over part of his new collection in advance or your viewing only," he says as I turn toward the women.

Then, they all at once drop their robes and walk toward us.

I immediately pin my attention on Crue. "You want this? Women walking around half naked?"

"It's not them I'm watching." And he isn't lying because his eyes have been on me the whole time. I turn back to the women as each of them comes to stand in front of me and gives me a full turn. When I glance at Crue, I see him whispering something to Dawson, who is now behind us. I focus back on the women, and one hands me a glass of champagne. I take it, but I am still confused by what's happening.

"What am I supposed to do?" I whisper to Crue.

Dawson laughs from behind me.

"Tell me which one you like best," Crue says.

Looking closer at the outfits, the women display, I say, "The lace with the leather nipple covers."

"Good. Your woman has expensive taste," Dawson says.

I twist my head to look at him. The words "Your woman" doesn't sit right with me. I'm not his woman. I'm a woman he's fucking. And now buying expensive lingerie for.

"How much?" I ask Dawson.

"The top is three thousand, and the bottom is two. If you want the whole combo with the stockings and garters, you're looking at just over six grand."

My mouth hangs open at that total. I have money, don't get me wrong. I tend to spend my money on work clothes, food, a few pieces of what I would consider nice lingerie, and nothing else. But my prices are in the hundreds.

"We will take one of every outfit. All in red," Crue says.

"How much is that?" I ask.

"At least fifty thousand," Dawson replies with a grin.

"Fuck."

"Yes, I plan to. While you're wearing them," Crue says as the women collect their robes and exit the bar. "Thanks, Dawson, you can go now." He waves Dawson off.

This is... too much.

Crue watches me pace back and forth. "Care for dinner, princess? My apartment is upstairs, and food is waiting for you."

I spin around to face him. "What are you doing?" I ask.

"Me?" He looks confused. "I'm planning to feed you, then I hope to fuck you later."

"And that's all? Because it seems like you have a motive."

"And what motive would that be?" he questions from where he lounges in the booth.

"You know what I'm talking about."

"No, I don't. You'll have to spell it out for me." His fingers tap on the table.

"You want me to marry you."

"I've never hid that motive."

"I will *not* become another wife. A stay-at-home, do-nothing-but-have-your-babies woman."

"Who said anything about staying at home?"

"I won't marry you."

Lazily, he says, "So you've said.

CHAPTER 32

Crue

A t the long wooden table that seats twenty, I sit opposite Rya.

"Why so far away, princess? Come sit next to me." I tap the chair beside me.

She shakes her head with a defiant smile, taking a mouthful of wine. Her hair is pinned up with a loose curl around her face. The low-cut, skin-tight black dress shows off every inch of her devastating body, including her peaked nipples.

"You asked me for dinner in your home and then forced me to dress in this. If you want to appreciate me, you can do it from a distance."

I smile, taking a swig of my whisky. It doesn't matter. It won't be long until I coax her onto my lap.

I've been hard since the moment she walked into the room.

Two servants stand to the side as the private chef comes out with a plate of steak for me and a lentil specialty for Rya that the chef told her he was excited to make.

"I cannot believe you live here by yourself." She scoffs like she doesn't believe what she is seeing while looking up at the chandelier. "The dining room is like an art exhibition in and of itself."

I cut into my steak. "Currently, Dominic, Angel, and my mother also occupy one wing of the penthouse."

Her eyes sparkle. "Is Angel here?"

"No, they're out for a few days."

She slumps back into her chair.

"Upset that it's just me, princess?"

"I've had better company."

I chuckle, and a small smile spreads on her lips. That fucking smile has my cock twitching with the memory of exactly what those lips felt like around it. I snap my fingers, indicating for everyone else to leave, including my two men.

She watches as they leave, but then her gaze shifts back to me as she wipes at her mouth, her meal barely touched.

I grab my glass of whisky and walk the length of the table to stand beside her.

She looks up at me through thick lashes. That heated gaze is fully aware of what I'm here for. My claim. The branding of what's mine.

Instead, she mentions, "The candles are a nice touch." She points to the multiple candles in the center of the table. "I didn't take you for a romantic."

I grab her jaw tightly, edging her gaze back up to me. As I lean down, my lips brush hers. "When have I ever given you that impression?"

I can sense her sarcastic smile. "When a boy buys a girl nice clothes and takes her to dinner... that's not usually what a sex buddy would do."

"I am *not* your sex buddy."

She laughs, her hot breath caressing me as she palms my cock. "So you don't want this?"

This woman is playing with fire.

"I want you." *Always.*

The heat in her gaze changes, and I press my tongue into her mouth. Possessive and demanding. It's been a few days since I've seen her, and I've barely been able to think about anything other than this.

I place my whisky to the side. Then I pick her up by the ass, and she wraps her legs around me. I push her food to the floor. The loud crash grabs her attention, but I snap her gaze back to me.

Fuck, those eyes.

That fiery spirit is so defiant against me even when her hands desperately slip to my belt. And then her hand finds its way to my gun.

I pull out the gun and he watches me inquisitively. He's a dangerous man.

One of his hands is around my throat, the other firmly bruising my thigh with his tight grip.

"Have you ever been shot before?"

"No. Are you going to shoot me, princess?" There's humor in his tone. Offended that he doesn't deem me a risk, so I raise the gun and pull the trigger. My heart rate accelerates as someone else screams. A wicked, cruel smile stretches his lips, and I can feel his cock pulse against my inner thigh.

He grabs my wrist and pins it forcefully against my back. I arch into him, a flood of exhilaration pulsing through me.

"Boss?" one of his men yells from outside the door.

"Stand down," he instructs with wickedness in his eyes. "I have to teach my new wife a lesson."

"I am not your—" He cuts me off as he pulls out his knife. I go still.

His hand slides up my leg, pushing my dress over my hip. "Have you ever been shot, princess?"

I'm both excited and suspicious. This man is lethal and a threat. He's proven that to me time and time again.

"No," I whisper. My grip on the gun becomes limp as Crue constricts my wrist.

My heart pounds in my chest. The adrenaline still spiking as he places the knife in my other hand. I eye it cautiously as I slowly release the gun.

"Have you ever cut someone, princess?"

My heart drops at the silent challenge. "No," I admit as I stare up at him, his imposing presence lingering over me like a devil reincarnated. I hate the control he has over me. Like his every little command while he has me in this state, I would follow.

"To be most effective, you cut across here." His thumb presses into my throat as he drags it across my skin. He watches the motion hungrily. "Or for a slow death..." His hand forcefully moves from my throat and trails down my stomach, causing my back to arch with anticipation.

How am I attracted to this?

His thumb comes to my inner thigh, drawing down and close to my pussy. "Here."

"And if I were to stab here?" I ask, pressing my hand to his chest.

"Then you better fucking run."

His words make my heart skip. I shouldn't be affected by this, but all control shatters as I try to reach up to him again. But he slams me down and, with efficient speed, removes his belt and drops his trousers.

He rips at the wrapper of the condom he pulled from his back pocket, and guides my legs until my calves are hitched over his shoulders. Appreciatively, he kisses my ankle with the anklet and his initial. Then, without warning, he slams into me. I try to buck as I adjust to his size, but his other hand pins me by the throat. He thrusts in deeper and takes my moans into his mouth.

I can't muffle my cries, which slowly turn into moans as air becomes thin with how tightly he constricts my throat. The table groans beneath us with every thrust, and things clatter to the floor. A spark of heat grabs my attention as flames erupt behind me from where the candles were clumsily knocked over.

"Cru—" He clenches tighter around my throat, taking my tongue for his, as he pounds into me, my body jarring with his heavy thrusts. Fear sets into my bones.

But the pleasure... *fuck, it feels so good.*

My eyes roll back in my head. Am I really willing to fucking die in a fire for this, though?

The lack of breath almost has me desperate, but I'm so fucking close. I bite at the bottom of his lip, drawing blood. A low growl escapes him.

Without thinking, I grab the knife and press it to his throat.

"Princess?" he whispers with a charmed smile. His hand slackens around my throat as his thrusts slow.

"You better make me come before that fire reaches me," I rasp as I nick at his throat, a small trail of blood left in its wake dribbles along his skin.

That primal growl escapes him again as he slams into me. I cry out in pain and pleasure as the fire spreads across the tablecloth. I'm out of my fucking mind, but I can't think of anything else.

That sweet spot he keeps hitting inside me, ramps up the pleasure. I press the knife to his skin, edging it toward his jugular, and his groan only emphasizes how much he fucking loves it.

With one more forceful thrust, he arches into me, hunching over me as he takes my lips. I scream his name into his mouth, the thrumming of my core finally spilling over. He picks me up, holding me like I'm something precious, as the flames spread over the tablecloth.

Smoke detectors scream and then water begins to sprinkle from the ceiling. The cold, hard realization has me shuddering as I follow the last wave of pure bliss.

Crue's hair dampens as he looks down to where I still hold the blade to his throat. "My dangerous vixen," he whispers with admiration.

With my men posted along the wall behind me, I sit and observe the patrons at the Ivanov Auctions. Unlike many here who wear a mask to cover their identity, I do not. Their attempt at anonymity is fruitless when it comes to me, as I know every single person in this room. Slimy Jim provided me with a list of the frequent patrons and their tastes, which is exactly the reason I came here tonight.

I sip on my whisky, my gaze locked on the woman who approaches my table.

"Mr. Monti, what a pleasure." Francesca Torrisi's smile doesn't reach her eyes. Perhaps because I put a bullet in her oldest brother's head a little over a year ago.

"It's a pleasure to finally meet with you, Francesca."

She's wearing a silver dress that shimmers with different colors as she moves. One of her men flanks her, offering a glass of champagne. She looks around the room, pinning onlookers with a glare.

"Sit with me," I say.

"Is that an invitation or a command?" she asks.

I offer an impolite smile. "Both."

She huffs and relieves her men. "It's fine."

She sits beside me, her hard, calculating gaze roaming the room.

"I have a proposition for you," I say.

She huffs out a laugh.

"I'm not the head of the Torrisi family. I can't offer you anything."

I lean closer to her, disgusted by her overly fragrant perfume. But perhaps that's because I've become accustomed to Rya's subtle potency. "And what if I could change that for you?"

Her gaze cuts to mine. She looks side to side skeptically to see who might be listening in. The lights are dim, and the auction is about to start. To others, it looks like an unfriendly exchange. And it very well might be, depending on her response.

"What makes you think I want to betray my family? My only nephew and remaining brother?"

"Two doesn't seem too many to cut down when you can become the heir, does it?"

I know what type of person Francesca is. She has specific tastes. A demand for power and recognition. Enough she's willing to kill for it, especially if she doesn't have to do the dirty work.

"What is this, some kind of trick?"

"Or an opportunity," I counter.

"Welcome, ladies and gents, to the Ivanov Auctions." Anya begins the night and we dispense with the pleasantries.

"You killed my brother," she hisses.

"And I plan on doing it to your other brother. Both stepped out of line. I wonder..." I pick up a stray piece of her hair. Some might consider it charming, but she and I both know it's a threat. "Are you as stupid as your siblings, or would being a boss create new terms in the way you have always wanted to run the family?"

A storm builds behind her eyes. "And what is it exactly you would want from me?"

I drop her hair and take a mouthful of my whisky. "Simple. An invitation to a party. Call it a peace offering." I'm the last person to ever offer peace, and she knows the party I'm referring to.

A spotlight lands on us, and Anya announces, "Our new member has offered a very generous piece to our collection tonight." She directs the attention to Dawson, who is standing center stage in a white suit. A few gasps erupt in the room. Dawson doesn't need an introduction, which is exactly why he is the perfect piece to display.

Francesca's gaze falls on him, and she licks her lips because Francesca Torrisi always wants things she can't have or shouldn't be able to obtain.

I lean back appreciatively as everything rolls into motion.

CHAPTER 35
Rya

I t's three in the morning when I feel Crue sliding into my bed.

"How did you get in? I changed the locks again." I grumble my complaint.

"Sorry, princess. I was late at work."

I don't even want to imagine what type of work he means. "Maybe you should get a nine-to-five job then."

He chuckles as he scoops me into him, his hand on my stomach with his chest against my back. His breath smells like whiskey. But there's an undertone of something else. I twist in his arms, his dark brown eyes intent on me as I groggily open mine.

I take another sniff. *Perfume*? And a lot of it. I push away from him and jump out of the bed.

"What the fuck?" I demand.

"What is it?" he asks. Confusion is an extremely strange expression to see on Crue. He rubs his chin while he tilts his head to the side.

"Why the fuck do you smell like women's perfume?"

His eyebrows furrow, and then he rolls his eyes. Actually, fucking rolls his eyes. I'm furious before he can even explain.

"I had a meeting tonight, and she was coated in the stuff."

"Did you fuck her?" I demand.

His eyes narrow. "Jealous, princess?"

Me? Fucking jealous? "We're just a quick fuck. What do I have to be jealous about? But I refuse to let you crawl into my bed when you've been with another woman. Get the fuck out! And do it *now!*"

"A quick fuck? Are you still pretending that's what this is?"

"Get the fuck out, Crue!"

"I'm not leaving." He makes a point of getting cozier. I'll be fucked if I'm going to let this man force me to leave my own home. I jump for my bedside table drawer and pull out the pistol that has sat in there unused since I first purchased this apartment. I point it at him, and he offers a dark tremble of laughter.

"Oh, princess. You don't want to make me mad."

"I don't think you should be saying that to the woman pointing a gun in your direction."

"You won't shoot me," he dares.

I arch an eyebrow. "Are you so sure? Do you forget whose daughter I am?"

He's silent for a moment. Contemplative. "I didn't sleep with her."

"And you sure as shit ain't sleeping with me tonight. Get *the fuck out*, Crue."

My hands are steady, but a wild storm of rage is licking at every inch of me. The thought of Crue with another woman? *Ridiculous.* I shouldn't be feeling this way over sex. Who cares if he slept with someone else? He isn't mine, and I don't fucking care. So why am I pointing a gun at him at the mere thought that he might have?

I can see the bulge in his pants. His heated stare of desire lights me up. And I hate how effective it is on me. How much I want it. "You are one sick fuck, you know that?"

He offers a dark smile.

I switch off the safety on the gun. "I mean it, Crue. Get out," I say again as I point the gun at his chest.

His smile falters. "Are you on your period?"

My mind goes blank and switches into unyielding rage. I aim for the bedside lamp on his side. It explodes beside him, and he doesn't so much as flinch while he continues to stare at me.

He blows out a whistle. "Well, I'll take that as a yes." He stands, his size filling the space. I keep the gun trained on him as I step back to my side of the bed while he circles it, and I point to the door.

"I will only let you go for tonight, princess. But I *will* teach you a lesson. You must know that it isn't very nice to point a gun at your husband."

"Get. The. Fuck. Out!" I yell after him as I hear the click of the door. My heart is pounding in my chest. I drop the gun on the bed, internally screaming that I actually had to use it.

Fuck. I look over to the broken porcelain beside my bed. I drop to my knees and begin to collect the larger pieces. *What the fuck is wrong with me?* My hands are now shaking as I pick up the pieces.

I don't care if Crue sleeps with anyone else. I try to convince myself, but the unsettling feeling lingers no matter how I argue it.

I will not *fall for someone like Crue Monti.* And the hard slap of reality at three in the morning sinks in.

I need to stop this now.

Because he is consuming me.

Entirely.

"You have got to be kidding me." I stare at the gift basket that was delivered five minutes ago to my office and now sits on my desk. The gigantic thing takes up at least half of the space.

The card reads...

Miss Ricci
I hope you don't find too much hardship in this challenging time. Periods must be difficult. Your body is your temple. And I will excuse your irrational behavior last night.
Get better soon,

Your soon-to-be husband

THE BASKET HOLDS VARIOUS THINGS. A bouquet of orchids, a box of chocolates, some bath bombs—even though I don't have a bathtub—and enough snack food to fill half my cupboard. *And... is that cough medicine?*

The thought of Crue acquiring any of these things on his own almost makes me laugh, but I'm sure he had one of his men organize this. And this basket seriously pisses me off. I look between it and the trash can. But it's bigger than the can.

My phone pings with another email.

Miss Ricci

I assume you have received your basket by now. Can we meet over dinner tonight if you are well enough for the occasion?

Reply.

Crue.

"You DEMANDING ASSHOLE!" I growl at my phone.

"Sorry?" Mr. Luca asks as he steps into my office.

I all but hide the phone as if caught with something illegal.

"Wow, that is an impressive basket." He whistles. "Belated birthday present?"

"No." I pick it up. "But it's too big to fit in the trash." So I drop it beside the can and hope one of the cleaners finds joy out of it.

His eyebrows knit together as he closes the door behind him. "I was hoping I could have a brief discussion with you today."

"Is everything all right?" I ask as I offer him the seat across from me, but he declines, so I make a point not to sit in mine. I tap my nail on the desk contemplatively.

"If it is about Brian's job, I told the board myself I won't step into the role until I've closed the Torrisi case."

He quirks a smile. "It's not about that."

Okay.

"I thought I should reach out and see how you're doing. I've been advised that perhaps you've been keeping unfavorable company as of late."

"Unfavorable company? You do realize that's my job, don't you?"

"I'm talking about the type you might have outside of work. That might jeopardize this firm."

My palm rests on the desk.

"Crue Monti, specifically."

"Are you about to give me a fatherly lecture as to what I should do in my spare time, Mr. Luca?"

He offers a flat smile. "Nothing fatherly about it. I'm simply ensuring it won't be a problem for the firm. We have clients who might not necessarily agree with your association with him."

"And what exactly are you under the impression my association with him is?"

He shrugs and licks his lips. A sign that the conversation is rolling in my favor. "He was here only a week ago. He has also been identified as the person who killed Brian."

"I had been advised that man was imprisoned and killed."

He offers another tight smile. "Right you are. I would hate for you to jeopardize this upcoming promotion because of *bad* company."

"Are you threatening me?" I ask.

Blood drains from his face. "No. I purely say it out of concern. I know some other board members have reservations about your relationship with Mr. Monti."

"Such as?" None of the other board members frequent the office as much as Mr. Luca, and I have the distinct impression that he's lying.

"I would rather not say. Please take it as a friendly concern, that's all."

Lucky for him, I'm not in the habit of making friends or being told what to do.

"You don't have to worry about Mr. Monti. I'm dealing with it." *One way or another.*

"Of course." He points to the open blue box in the basket. I purposefully ignored it before. "Those are beautiful pearls."

Had he known part of that note also mentioned the matching piece Crue would give me later as a pearl necklace, he might not have been so quick to comment.

"I'm sure the donations box will love them," I add with a tight smile.

Asshole.

CHAPTER 37

Rya

Angel's eyes grow wide. "You shot at him?"

I wave my hand. "Not at him. The lamp beside his face."

Dominic covers his mouth in attempt to hide the chuckle. "Fuck, Rya, you have bigger balls than I thought."

"I will take that as a compliment. Thank you very much," I say, popping a french fry in my mouth. Angel had a craving for a Five Guys burger, so here we are, with two shady men standing near the entrance—a dead giveaway that no one should fuck with Angel or Dominic.

She slurps on the thick shake and looks at Dominic. He averts his gaze. "Dominic," she warns.

"What, woman? You know he gets mad if I tell

other people his business."

She rests her hand on her stomach. "I'm pretty sure anything to do with Rya *is* his business."

He sighs. "All I'm going to say is, I was with him two nights ago, and he definitely did not have sex with anyone. And I don't think he has intentions of going anywhere else anytime soon."

A cold relief washes over me, and I hate how that makes me feel. That sense of lightness, but also dread and embarrassment that I reacted in such a way, linger. That I let Crue crawl under my skin.

"He's obsessed with you, Rya," Angel says what Dominic could not.

"It's just sex. *Was* just sex."

"*Was?*" she asks.

"I'm done with it. I got Crue out of my system, and now I can continue with my life."

"Was Crue a part of the discussion?" she asks warily. She and Dominic share a glance.

"He didn't need to be. He doesn't own me."

They share another look. They might be under Crue's control, but I sure as hell am not. Nor will I ever be.

"Is that why you're hiding out?"

"I'm not hiding out." I nonchalantly shrug, tapping my sharp nail on the table. "The Torrisi case is coming to a close. I have a lot of things riding on this case. Crue is a distraction."

"Have we been a distraction?" she asks quietly, rubbing her hand on her stomach.

"No. Of course not. I'm so happy you're here."

"Only two more weeks, though," she reminds me.

Again, Dominic and Angel share another look as if they are in on something that I am not.

"Can't you convince him to go back home with you?" I ask Dominic.

He snorts. "Have you ever tried to convince Crue of anything?"

I sit back in my chair. *Touché.*

Angel leans over and reaches for my hand. It's uncomfortable, but I don't pull away. "You might be convincing yourself that Crue is out of your system, but I don't think you're out of his."

"If you ever will be," Dominic grumbles under his breath.

"This is not the life I want to be a part of. I have always been very clear about that."

And the further away I am from Crue Monti, the better because I feel like I can breathe and think for myself again.

And more importantly, figure out how I'm going to avoid him.

CHAPTER 38

Crue

As I stare up at the hotel that Rya checked into two nights ago after she accused me of sleeping with another woman, I sigh. My little vixen is on the run, and I'm almost disappointed in her. I never thought she'd flee her own home. But what's more disappointing is she didn't think I could find her so easily.

Dominic is standing beside me. He drops his smoke and puts it out with his heel. "I don't think you should go in tonight. Sometimes women need space."

I shoot him a glare. "That woman is my soon-to-be wife. She should be by my side at all times. None of this cat and mouse shit."

Although I do enjoy the chase.

But I have a job tonight, so I slip back into the car's

back seat. Dominic starts the engine and takes off. I can sense he's looking at me through the rearview mirror.

"We leave in two weeks. The families back home will want answers and a wedding," he reminds me.

"I know," I reply firmly. I don't need reminding of my deadline.

Tentatively, he adds, "It doesn't have to be her. It could be anyone."

I glare at him. He shrugs his shoulders, remaining silent this time.

I know it could be anyone else.

But it has always been her.

Rya Ricci *will* be my wife.

CHAPTER 39
Rya

Dear Miss Ricci
Your attendance is required this weekend.
Reply.
Crue

M y hands shake in rage.

Goddammit! I received that email one minute before a delivery was made to my hotel suite door. A large white box sits on my bed. So he knows I've been holed up in the hotel for the last week. And worse, he still expects me to be his little doll on display.

When will this man get a hint or, at the very least, understand the term "ghosting"?

I sigh, curiosity getting the better of me as I open the box. I only lasted an hour. Inside is a long black dress with a slit up the outer leg. The front is low-cut. There are pearl earrings and a necklace to match the dress. He must have known I donated the last earrings. A pair of black Louis Vuitton heels finish off the outfit.

I wonder what event it might be that he so desperately needs me to attend. Knowing him, it could be as simple as going through a takeout drive-through to order, and he would still want me to wear something like this.

"No, thank you."

I close the box and throw it under the bed. I can't. And it's not exactly hiding any more if he knows where I am. I'm one of the most powerful lawyers in New York. So why the fuck do I feel so weak against this man?

He is obsessed. And I'm trying my hardest to flee because I know he is no good for me. Time with him would be nothing but a beautiful disaster.

I walk into the main room and take a seat at the dining table, where my laptop is still open and waiting for me. Friday is the day I give my closing statements on the Torrisi case in court. And then, on Monday, the verdict will be announced. This is what I should be focusing on. This is the biggest case of my career. So, anything Monti or otherwise, I push away and ignore even if I have to change to another hotel in the meantime.

CHAPTER 40
Crue

It was hot and fascinating watching Rya grow jealous. But now she hasn't replied to my emails, which I won't tolerate.

I'm not at all surprised by how effective Dawson is. Francesca Torrisi sent a personalized invitation to their latest party celebrating Andreas's fiftieth birthday. She had, of course, bid the most for Dawson's company for one night. They've seen each other twice now.

Dawson hands me the invitation. "I'm surprised she didn't offer you an invitation."

He smiles. "Who do you think is escorting her?"

As expected, he takes a seat across from me in my office. "Do you think it's smart forcing Rya to go? She's working on his nephew's case."

I take a sip of whisky. "Rya's my wife. Where I go, she goes."

Dawson lets out a small whistle. "You, my friend, are not so good with women. And she isn't your wife."

"Excuse me?" I grit out.

He raises a brow. "I'm just suggesting that if a woman doesn't return to her home in a week and switches from not one but two hotels, she *is* actively avoiding you."

My knuckles turn white. "I don't care what you suggest."

He nods in agreement. "That much is clear."

I take a puff of my cigar, watching the surveillance footage I have of Rya's empty apartment.

Why won't she just submit to me?

Am I giving her too much freedom?

I crack my neck from side to side. But she's given me no other choice. She *will* be going to that party with me. So the Torrisi family knows how much they fucked up when they pointed a gun in her direction.

CHAPTER 41

Rya

The judge closes the case. The last of the questions and answers reported. The jury and the other party have already made their leave.

When I walk out, I'm greeted by numerous cameras and reporters. I flash a tentative smile.

"Miss Ricci, how are you and the defendant feeling at this time?"

I quickly shoot Matteo a look. He knows not to speak outside of the court. "My client and I are confident that what the jury has seen is fair reasoning as to my client's predicament with his previous friend. My client was only able to defend himself, and although our condolences go out to the family for their loss, my client is also dealing with severe trauma, for which we have already drafted a plan to facilitate his mental needs."

"And what of the new accusations of Matteo Torrisi having recently killed four other known gang members?"

My smile tightens. "Those are, of course, accusations that have already been discussed in the court room. Although the evidence isn't clear, and I reiterate the strange timing of events considering the large deposit made into the opposing party's bank account within a day of this incident, I hope the jury will find fair judgment in the matter."

Why? Because I instructed Andreas Torrisi to anonymously deposit that amount immediately to take the heat off his nephew's case.

The shine of a watch catches my eye, and my stomach drops. Leaning against his car is Crue, puffing on a cigar. Even with him wearing dark sunglasses, I know his gaze is on me.

"That's all the questions I have time for today." I dismiss them and walk in the opposite direction. *Fuck.* He can't be here. I can't have the press catching wind of our association. Not with this heated case still going on in the courtroom.

Security pushes the press back as we take our leave,

and it's only a matter of time before they give up and move to the second family.

"Where are we going?" Matteo asks.

"Shut up and follow me," I hiss.

He grumbles a complaint but does as I say.

We walk a few blocks before I turn into an alleyway. It's the most secure place I can find for dealing with a fucking hell hound who won't give up the damn pursuit.

I see three shadows fall behind us when we step into the alleyway. That's when I cross my arms and spin around, nothing but venom laced in my tone as I say *his* name, "Crue."

"Princess." He lights another cigar and casually slips one of his hands into his pocket. "You've been avoiding me."

"Yeah, how nice of you to notice."

"I sent you an email."

"Numerous emails, actually," I correct. "I'm busy with work. I can't join you for your little escapade."

He points the gun at Matteo, and my stomach sinks.

"What the fuck, man?" Matteo squeaks, lifting his hands.

"What are you doing?" I hiss, stepping in front of my client. My heels click against the uneven pavement.

I shift my gaze to Dominic and the other guy flanking Crue, but they're expressionless. Not even Dominic is showing any emotion now, and that's highly unusual.

"Princess, you seem to have deleted my email again. Your presence is required. And if your client is dead, then you don't have a case to manage."

"You *cannot* be fucking serious," I spit.

"Do you have any idea who my uncle is, man!" Matteo shouts over my shoulder.

"Shut the fuck up," I tell Matteo, and he seems almost shocked.

"You seem rather coddled if your uncle hasn't informed you of who *I am*."

"Oh, for fuck's sake. We are not doing a pissing competition in this alleyway."

"So I'll pick you up tonight at eight? You really brought this upon yourself, princess."

"What part of *no* do you not understand?"

He cocks a half smile. It's beautiful, wild, and wicked. "Nobody says no to me. Not even you, wifey."

"Wifey?" Matteo asks.

"I am *not* your wife! But that's *not* the fucking point," I scream. "You are so fucking frustrating, you know that?"

Crue shrugs nonchalantly. "Do you want that next fat paycheck or not?"

I narrow my gaze on him. I'm still standing in front of the boy as Crue takes deliberate steps toward me.

"You forget I can kick you in the balls. And I want to, really fucking hard right now," I hiss.

That elegant smile remains as he tips the muzzle of the gun under my jaw. And I don't know why, but I feel no fear, even though I know I should. There is something seriously messed up with me.

"You won't shoot me," I say confidently.

"No, but there are other ways to break someone." His lips are a heated breath away from mine, and my thighs clench in anticipation. I could scream at myself with the frustration I am feeling. *Why can I* not *pull free of this man?*

"I will pick you up at eight. Don't be late." He kisses me, the gun still under my jaw as his tongue demands mine. My body leans into him as if this last week away from him was more a curse than a blessing. I pull away, yanking myself free of his magnetism.

Fuck, I hate that he knows everything I like.

He chuckles. "And don't worry, princess. I have your new address."

Crue turns to Matteo. "Good luck with the court case. I hope it buys you a few more days of freedom."

"What the fuck is that supposed to mean?" Matteo

throws his hands in the air, and I pin him with a stare. Why is this kid so fucking dense? Does he really not understand when a predator has him cornered?

Maybe I should ask myself the same question.

Well, fuck.

Looks like I'm getting dressed up for an event after all.

CHAPTER 42
Rya

Beautiful.

That's the word I would use to describe the dress and minor details that hug the shape of my body. It infuriates me to acknowledge Crue has good taste.

I'm late. *Again*. Purposefully.

I step out of the elevator and through the hotel lobby. Numerous gazes are on me as I hold my head high and walk toward the man that most cautiously avoid. He's in a black suit with a black dress shirt beneath. His gaze rakes from my heels up until those molten brown eyes collide with mine. Crue licks his lips and looks like he's ready to devour me right here, right now, and damn the consequences.

But instead, he says, "You're late."

"And you're insufferable."

His tension relieves slightly when he drops his shoulders as a devastating smile slowly spreads on his lips. I'm certain I am the only one who can be late and manage a smile from this man. No matter how cruel and cunning it is.

He holds out his elbow.

I ignore it and step toward his men. "So, where are we going?" I don't even have to see to know he's watching me. "Crue, stop staring at my ass. This is not that type of night."

I hear his chuckle from behind me. Crue's hand reaches around my stomach, pulls me into him, and his breath is hot against my neck. "But isn't it always that type of night?"

"Not for you and me anymore." I push away, trying my hardest to hold my cold, hard expression. One I have honed for years in the court room. No matter how much my body hungers for him, if I sleep with Crue again, I might as well be admitting my own defeat.

One of his men opens the back door for me, but I open the front passenger door and slide in that seat instead. The three men look between one another, stiffening.

"It's fine," Crue insists. When the driver-side door

opens, Crue climbs in, and a cold shiver runs down my spine.

"What?" I turn around to see his two bulky men now sitting in the back.

Crue's hand grips my leg through the revealing slit. "Don't test me tonight, princess," Crue warns.

"Don't get your alpha asshole shit on with me tonight," I throw back.

He stares at my lips, his grip tightening on the steering wheel, turning his fingers white. "Those filthy lips."

I look away and out the window. The problem is that I can't do anything to resist that look, or him, and even his grip on my thigh is a slow-burning torture, but I pretend to be unfazed by it.

CHAPTER 43

Rya

When we approach the estate, I pale. "Are you kidding me?"

Crue says nothing as we motor up the property's long driveway thirty minutes outside the city. I know exactly whose home this is.

"You cannot seriously be taking me to the Torrisi's house while I'm mid-case with them. Do you know how bad that looks for me if I'm seen being chummy with them?"

"Chummy?" he says as if that's the most offensive part of what I have just said. "Would it not be seen as flattering that you have such a great relationship with your clients?"

"No, I'll look like a sellout."

"Consider it an opportunity. You can even hand

out your business card. I'm sure there are plenty of criminals here who need to be defended in court."

Crue pulls up at the entrance, and I turn to him, doing all I can to hide my trembling fury. This man knows exactly how to push my buttons. To make me go from zero to one hundred with only a few words.

"Why are we even here?"

He pulls an invitation out from his suit jacket. "I received an invitation, of course."

I narrow my gaze on the invitation. No, these families have bad blood between them. More factually, Crue has bad blood with most people unless they're like the majority who fear him and do as he says.

My door is opened for me by a hostess who smiles brightly. "Welcome to the celebration of Andreas Torrisi's fiftieth birthday. On your right, please take a welcome gift with the freshly branded Torrisi whisky line and a special surprise."

I shudder at her rehearsed lines.

Crue steps around the car and offers his hand to me. I consider refusing it, but I know better in a social situation such as this. Whether it be with my father or Crue, I will just have to smile through the entire evening until it's over.

"Why am I really here?"

"Because you will be my wife and will soon represent the Monti family," he replies simply.

"We agreed you would stop with that."

"We agreed I would stop asking."

I grit my teeth and smile as another staff member tries to hand me a white and gold bag. Inside, there is a bottle of whiskey and what looks to be a bag of... "Is that cocaine?" I ask Crue incredulously.

"Looks like it will be a lively party after all." He declines the offering.

"And seriously, a whisky line?"

The moment we step into the monstrous mansion, a waitress offers us two flutes of champagne.

"Easy to hide behind a business for another business," he explains.

I roll my eyes as I take a mouthful of the bubbly alcohol. The cocaine was probably bought from the same warehouse.

I down the glass completely, and he watches me with a half-cocked smile.

"What?" I demand as I place the empty glass on the tray of a passing waitress.

"You haven't changed one bit."

"Excuse me?" I scoff, my nails biting into the sleeve over his wrist.

"The first time I met you when you were sixteen, you downed a flask, then chased it with wine."

I feel stunned for a moment that he remembers that long ago. The memory for me is vague at best. But instead, I shrug as I collect another flute and say, "Turns out I have more to drink about now than I did back then."

He chuckles as we walk through the house, where hundreds of people are laughing and smoking cigars, drinking, and some are already feral off God only knows what drugs.

In the backyard, there are even more people spread out. Women in bikinis and shirtless men jump into and laze around the pool. Others are polished in their finest as they idly chat at tables where trays of food and drinks are being offered.

I flick a glance at Crue's men, who not-so-casually blend in as they walk behind us. But we're not the only ones with security. Despite being at a party, everyone is on edge. Power ripples through the atmosphere. It reminds me of the parties I was forced to join with my father and all the unruly men who made me uncomfortable with the way they looked at me, even at sixteen. But I doubt with Crue at my side, they will consider looking at me twice. And that's not so much a comfort as it is a warning.

Finally, a familiar face appears through the crowd. Dawson is wearing his usual stark-white suit as he escorts a woman who looks to be in her mid-forties. I don't need to know her name to realize she's a Torrisi. Her sharp green gaze pins me with a stare and then moves to Crue.

"Crue, you made it after all," she says with a smile that doesn't reach her eyes. And then she turns to me. "And I hear I have a lot to thank you for, bailing out my foolish nephew for his misdeeds."

Nephew. So that means she's Andreas's sister. "It's not yet a won case. But, yes, I'm feeling confident. Rya Ricci." I offer my hand.

Her eyebrows shoot up. "How untraditional not to take the husband's name." I'm taken aback by that comment, but don't let it show on my face. She curls her hand around mine. "Francesca Torrisi. I hope you enjoy your evening. There's always plenty to see." A mischievous twinkle dances in her gaze as she looks at Crue.

And there's something in her stare that I feel uneasy about. I push down that feeling. No, Crue is a powerful man. Of course, people are attracted to that. And I hate myself even more that it's a misgiving of mine because I shouldn't care.

"How about you take a seat with me, Rya." Dawson thankfully draws my attention.

"Shall I take you to Andreas?" Francesca asks Crue.

His gaze flashes between Dawson and me, a prickly sensation crawling up my skin.

Crue leans in, his kiss feather-light against my cheek. "I'll be back, princess. Enjoy the party while I'm gone."

Dawson offers his elbow to me. I take it, unable to avoid looking over my shoulder at Crue. I notice that only one of his men follows him, and the other sticks with me and Dawson. I can't help but think how calculated this all feels. But when it comes to Crue, what else is to be expected?

"You need to find new friends, you realize that, right?" I say to Dawson as he takes me to a small table, slightly more secluded and quieter than those in the middle of the patio. A gentle water fountain trickles behind us, which would normally be calming, but the noise only aggravates me further.

He chuckles as he offers his flute to mine in cheers.

I like Dawson. There's a remarkably charming and calming element to him. But that's what makes him dangerous. It's a trained façade. A man like Dawson, who is associated with someone like Crue, comes from a place where questions should not be asked.

"If memory serves correctly, you seem to like my friend very, very much," he says.

I scoff. "I like his body very, very much."

Dawson goes quiet for a moment, contemplative even as he looks over his shoulder. "You do know he's in love with you?"

What feels like a rash immediately climbs up my skin, and I cough, enduring another mouthful of champagne as I wave someone over for another.

"Someone like Crue doesn't know how to love," I say as I swap out the empty glass for a full one.

He considers me. "I'm not going to argue with that. But he has never brought anyone to these types of events, representing him in this way."

"Please," I huff. "The problem with men like Crue is they can bring anyone to these events and still leave with whoever they want."

"He might have brought women on his elbow, but none of whom anyone remembered their names after the event was done. And boy, did he have a type."

"A type?"

"Oh, you know. Caramel blonde, light eyes, pretty face." His gaze locks with mine. And there's no disputing the fact that Dawson is beautiful, but his insinuation unnerves me more.

"Trust me when I say I know the difference between love and infatuation," Dawson adds.

"He would kill you if he knew you were telling me this."

He shrugs nonchalantly as he eyes other partygoers. "Then let's hope you're good at keeping secrets. And I'm doing this more for my friend because I know he will burn this city alive if he can't have you."

And that's what terrifies me about Crue Monti.

Because he has the power to do exactly that and more.

CHAPTER 44

Crue

I sit across from Andreas in a private room.

We lounge on leather couches, and there is a coffee table with lines of cocaine between us. Fire is crackling in the fireplace beside us. Where he has four bodyguards behind him, I only have one. And although this is his home, I lean back and cross one leg over the other, comfortably in control.

"Help yourself." Andreas offers the cocaine as he leans over and snorts a line.

"No, thank you. I already get a portion of the profit in what you sell. I have no need to try it."

Andreas gives me a tight smile. "Is our current agreement something you want to address?"

I shrug and take a mouthful of the Torrisi whisky. It has a sharp after bite that's not to my liking. "Not just yet. I came to address another matter."

I watch as he grinds his teeth. It must be so easy for him to envision shooting me down right here and now. But he would be nothing without what my great-grandfather provided his family before and what I so generously allow them to have now.

"What matter might that be?" he asks while lighting a cigar and brushing back his gelled hair.

"Two weeks ago, someone attempted a hit on me outside one of my establishments."

"I'm sorry to hear that. But that could come from any family here in New York. You've ruffled some feathers since arriving," he says, stating facts.

I pull a tight smile that's anything but friendly. "I also had your nephew's lawyer with me at the time, who could have been collateral damage in the process."

It takes him a moment to register that fact. "This is about Miss Ricci? You know I wouldn't want any harm to come to her. Why would we? She is the only lawyer who could possibly get my nephew out of the shit he found himself in."

"And yet when I track it back, a man named Morpheus said it was the Torrisi family that called in the hit. He told me this right before I shot him in the head."

Realization dawns on his face.

"So now we have a predicament."

He grows paler, but his eyes begin to dilate from the drugs. One of his men reaches for his gun, but Andreas puts his hands up. "No. There's no need for that. I swear to you, I have no idea who called in that hit, but I will find out and deal with them myself."

I click my tongue. "Ah... but I don't think that will be enough. You see, I've grown rather fond of Miss Ricci, considering she is to be my wife."

Andreas turns a shade of green.

"You have one week," I say, standing. And for the first time in my life, I've been diplomatic.

"O-one week for w-what?" he stutters.

"I want the head of the person who organized the hit on me. I will also send documentation over for you to sign that for the next year, I will receive fifty-one percent of all profits from this disgusting whisky. Oh, and of course, the drugs you ship through that warehouse."

"Fifty-one percent?" he says, shocked at the amount.

"And if it isn't signed, I will kill every single person in your family. Your sister. Your wife. And your mistress with your six-year-old little Whinny. Cute kid, by the way."

"How do you know about—"

I glare over my shoulder. "And I think Miss Ricci deserves a *very* generous bonus for her hard work on your shithead nephew."

Casually, I throw my glass and its contents into the fireplace. Flames erupt on contact. I wait for him to turn on me. For some action to take place. But instead, he starts yelling at his men to get busy on my orders.

"Oh, by the way." I linger at the door. "Happy Birthday. I hope you make it to your next."

CHAPTER 45

Crue

"Y ou let her get this drunk?" I growl furiously to Dawson.

Rya's chuckling to herself, a glass of champagne clutched in her hand. "You know, I was always told to be a good girl at these events," she says to Dawson as if they've been friends forever. "Don't say too much. Sit tall. Be in your room by ten. If you hear a noise, hide behind your bodyguard." She points to me and snorts. "But who needs a guard when you always have a seriously pissed-off Monti at your side? I mean, seriously, look at him. He always looks like he's just bitten into a lemon."

I guarantee Dawson an intimate death with my gaze alone. He tries to pry the drink from her. "No offense, but how do you try to force her to do anything when she doesn't want to?"

He hands her over to me. Well, shit, at least she can still stand on her own. Sort of.

"Are you having a mental break down?" I ask her.

She stands tall. Deadly serious as her gaze lands on me. "I don't know, maybe I'm on my period again."

Dawson barely hides his smirk as he quickly cuts off his chuckle.

"Dawson," I grit out.

"You've got it rough, Crue. I'll give you that."

"I need to pee," Rya announces.

I tilt my head to the sky with a silent prayer and curse under my breath. Of all the things I thought she might have gotten up to, this was not one of them. Nor would I condone her behavior. And I would certainly cut down anyone who dared take away from her fun.

"Crue, take me to the bathroom," she whines, grabbing my elbow.

I have never dealt with this side of Rya.

And I've seen her drink a lot.

"How much did she drink?" I ask Dawson. He looks at the remains of three bottles of champagne.

"I only had four glasses," he says.

"We were D and M-ing," Rya says as if answering an unspoken question.

"Okay, princess." I try not to laugh at her state because, well, smashed Rya is... adorable? There's a word I never thought I would use to describe this venomous vixen.

"I'm going to take this woman to the bathroom, and then we'll go."

"No, I don't want to go." She pouts.

Dawson is hiding another smile.

"Fuck off, Dawson."

He excuses himself as Francesca approaches us. I lead Rya to a private bathroom at the back of the house and closest to the pool. Music floods the room.

"That's a nice bathtub," she says in admiration as we stumble into the bathroom. "Remember those bath bombs you bought me? I threw them out."

She stumbles over to the toilet and drops her panties before she sits.

"Wow, Rya," I say, looking the other way.

"Oh, don't be so weird about it. Everyone has to pee."

I chuckle. One thing I'm sure of is when I finally make this vixen my wife—and I *will* make her my wife —I will definitely be entertained. How strange it is to see this side of her. Behind the lawyer and the suit, I consider that this fiery spirit still wants to be set free. Something I could offer her when she accepts my hand.

She finishes her business and then washes her hands. Rya looks at herself in the mirror, brushing her hair from side to side until it falls the way she wants it to.

I come up behind her, wrapping my arm around her waist and making eye contact with her in the mirror. Her drunk gaze promises everything sober Rya hides. But here, right at the surface, is this wild, beautiful version of her leaking at the edges to escape.

So why won't she accept what I'm offering when I can give her the world?

CHAPTER 46

Rya

"We should get you home." His voice rakes down my body like every inch is on fire. Hot and in need of him. I downed those drinks all night, more irritated by my conflicting feelings. Every time I look at him, I hate him but need him all the same, like it's my next fucking breath. He's like my own personal heroin.

But nothing good will come from us being together.

In this moment... there is no past or future... there is only the now.

It always feels like that with Crue. I only want to focus on the now, damning myself with the consequences the next day.

I twist in his arms and wrap my arms around his

neck. When I do, I can feel his cock hardening. "You like my touch," I say with a flirty smile.

"I like those filthy lips of yours," he admits as he brings his finger up to rub the red on my lips.

"These lips?" I whisper as I drop to my knees. I undo his belt with efficiency before curling my hand beneath the weight of his cock and setting it free. It's beautiful and inviting. All things Crue—divine, larger than life, and delicious.

I wrap my lips around his cock, the light flavor of salt spiking over my tastebuds as I take him. I drag my teeth along his flesh, and he hisses. The pulse in his cock throbbing on my tongue. I like the way he feels and tastes.

He tries to knot his hands in my hair, but I slap them away and look up at him. "You will do as you're told."

Crue grabs my throat and pulls me up to his level. I can barely breathe, but I yearn for his reward.

"I don't get told to do anything."

I fist his cock, and his head falls back slightly. I place my other hand on his cheek as if I am inviting him in for a secret, and I say against his lips, "But you will for me."

His eyes heat with a warning. "Careful, princess." His hand cups me over my dress, and his clever fingers dance along my sweet spot that has already come to life for him.

"What do you need from me?" he asks.

"Good sex, obviously," I purr.

"Because I'm in your top two?"

I poke my tongue in my mouth. "You're still striving for that, huh? Maybe you need some more practice."

His smile is slow and sensual. "We can practice all you like."

I'm suddenly conscious of a nauseating swirl in my stomach.

His face drops. "Princess, what's wrong?"

"I feel sick," I say, suddenly in a panic. "Like really sick."

"What do you—"

I can't shove him out of the way fast enough and vomit on his shoes then I all but crawl back to the toilet. After the case today and coming straight here, I realize I never had the chance to eat. And three or so bottles of champagne are not my friend.

CHAPTER 47
Crue

S he barely missed vomiting on my cock. I've been a part of some pretty messed up shit, and I've dealt with my fair share of blood and gore all over my body, but this—having my dick out and someone throwing up on my shoes—is new. And something I never want to revisit again.

Her head is pillowed in my lap as I rub my thumb over her shoulder. My driver has kept his gaze on the road the entire time. Instead of returning to the hotel, I take her to her apartment.

I want to take her back to my place, but with the fuss of my mother, Angel, and Dominic there, I decide to give her what she's been demanding... space.

I wonder when I became attached to her. I've only ever known obsession, and I'm still telling myself that's all it is. But with Rya, I'm entertained by her quick wit and, well, situations such as tonight. And her body drives me cruelly insane. Once I had my first taste, I haven't been able to stop.

I don't know anything about love.

But not having Rya by my side is not an option.

And there isn't much time left for her to feel like she has that choice.

But for now, I'll let her sleep.

CHAPTER 48
Rya

Today, I woke with a seriously bad headache and vague memories of the night before. I grumble a complaint to myself. *What had I been thinking?* It's been so long since I dropped my guard like that. Was it because I felt safe with Dawson? Or maybe I really am having a mental breakdown.

It's now been over a month since Crue stepped into my life again, and it's been nothing but chaos ever since. My pussy pulses with regret. Not only did I give in to him, but I initiated it. And I still didn't get laid.

"Kill me now," I mumble into my pillow.

"I think the hangover is doing a pretty good job of that," Angel says as she walks into my room with a glass of juice and what smells like burned toast.

I look between her and the toast, my head throbbing. "I can see your cooking skills haven't improved."

"Shut up." She laughs as she waddles further and sits at the end of my bed as I lean against the headboard and bring my knees up to my chest. A quick swirl encouraging another nauseous wave.

"Wow, I haven't seen you this rough since my fifteenth birthday, and we drank that entire bottle of vodka."

The memory brings another twinge of nausea.

"Any demons you're particularly running away from this time?" she asks.

We both know what I'm running away from. "Not demons. *A* demon," I correct as I take the glass of juice.

"Well, that same demon took care of you all night. And I'm certain he burned those shoes the moment I arrived to take his place. He had to deal with some work."

I hold my head in my hands. "This is the exact opposite of how I want to feel for court tomorrow."

"So let's have a Netflix day and order takeout." She awkwardly stands, holding her back as she does. The more I see her, the more heavily pregnant she seems.

"Only one more week until you go, huh?" And I feel sad knowing she'll be leaving. I've gotten used to her being here.

"Don't go all sentimental on me now." Angel laughs.

"Not even while hungover," I promise.

Sentimentality is *not* my thing. And yet, when I remove the blanket, it reveals that Crue has once again clasped the anklet with his initial around my ankle. It isn't so much sentiment as it is an unnegotiable possession.

CHAPTER 49

Rya

A wave of pure adrenaline washes over me as the jury and judge award my winning case. That's why I love this job. That recognition is the best along with the hefty paycheck.

The time for resting will come, as it always does, but for some reason, I feel even more exhilarated than usual by this win. I've been working so hard on this case, and despite how chaotic my life has been with Crue in tow, I won. *Again.*

I humbly answered questions and thanked reporters for their dedication to the case, and now I sit across from Andreas and Matteo in my office. Luckily, I hadn't seen either of them at the party two nights ago. Not that it changed anything. As of this afternoon, I'm done with the Torrisi family.

"Fuck yeah. I'm a free man," Matteo celebrates.

I tap my nail on the desk thoughtfully. "Just don't mess it up."

Andreas has been quiet since our last meeting. The way he's been looking at me, it's as if I've grown a second head. I thought he would be much more high-spirited, as opposed to how he now stares miserably at his nephew.

"Come on, Uncle Andreas, isn't this great?" Matteo asks.

"It is. Of course, it is," Andreas says, snapping out of his stupor. "Thank you for all your help, Miss Ricci. We won't be any trouble for you going forward."

I shake his hand, a little confused by his words. "Well, if you need my services, you know you'll be paying for them," I joke.

He seems to pale. "As in because my services aren't cheap," I explain, feeling awkward as I pull my hand back.

"Oh, of course." He offers a polite enough smile. "I'll be depositing the final amount owed this afternoon. And if there is anything you need from me or the Torrisi family, please don't hesitate to ask."

"Okaaay," I say, still confused by his behavior. *Did he snort too much of his own product again?*

"Come on, Matteo, let's not take any more of Miss

Ricci's time." He grabs his nephew by the back of the neck and basically shoves him out of the office as he flees after him. Matteo looks as baffled as I feel.

Okay, that was the first time I've ever had someone run out of my office after winning a case.

A ping comes from my phone. I check it and see I have a new email from Crue and an unread message from my mother, so I read the message from my mother first.

> Mom: Congrats on the win, sweetie! I've had an idea. I need to return to Italy for a few weeks. You should come back with me. Take some time off before you accept that new promotion of yours.

ITALY? That's a random invitation, and I wonder what Mom has back in Italy.

I check my emails.

Dear Miss Ricci

Congratulations on your win. We'll celebrate accordingly.
I'll pick you up at seven. It's the least you can do after ruining my shoes.
Don't be late.
Reply.
Crue

I SMILE AT THE SCREEN, although I know I shouldn't. But the thought of seeing Crue's face when I vomited on his shoes while his cock was hanging in the wind is hilarious. And truthfully, how can I say no to him now? At the very least, I can give him one more night to make up for that little transgression. But, of course, and as usual, I don't reply. Knowing that Crue Monti always keeps to his word.

Without permission, he will still be at my door at seven.

And I'll be late.

While sitting on the couch, I finish watching another news channel. Something I've been doing frequently in recent weeks so I can watch Rya on screen. I knew she would win, but pride touches me in the way you can see her eyes dance with adrenaline from the win. Her fire blazes through, making me hard as fuck when I imagine this powerful woman on her knees in front of me.

"You can come in now." I permit Dominic to join me. I light a victory cigar as I turn the television off.

"She won then?" Dominic asks as he enters and tosses documents on my desk.

"Naturally," I say around my cigar.

I look over the documentation. One report is from Slimy Jim. Rya's mother ceased the need for his services. That didn't sit well. Most with a curious mind don't stop hunting for answers until they are satisfied. And I very much doubted Rya's mother is the type to drop something. I can confirm that she and Rya are similar in that sense. But perhaps when she understood who exactly I am, she thought it best not to dig up anything she couldn't handle, including my wrath. She is a smart woman, after all.

The second set of documents were ones I'd been anticipating for some time. "So it's all ready now?"

Dominic replies, "Yes. The countdown is on. It's definitely going to create a stir here with the families."

"Then it's lucky I'm the best at damage control. And sometimes it's simply best to wipe everything out so there's nothing to recover or left to squash." I made that mistake with the Torrisi family once. Sometimes, cutting off one head isn't enough. You have to cut them all. My attendance at the party ensured I got everything I wanted from them.

I flick to the third report.

Dominic's gaze lands on it. "Are you sure she'll go through with this?"

I kick up an arrogant smile. "She'll have no choice."

CHAPTER 51

Rya

As expected, Crue is on time. And I chose to sit on my couch for another fifteen minutes in order to be late.

As I greet the driver and slide into the back seat, I can see that Crue is fuming. "Princess," he all but growls.

"Yes?" I ask sweetly.

"Were you just sitting up there watching TV?"

"Of course not. I was very conscious of what you might think about what I was wearing." I offer my best fake pout. "Do you not like it?"

He grabs the back of my neck and pulls me into him, his growl a hot flash on my mouth. "I told you *not* to be late."

"And I told you to leave me alone."

"Hmm," he hums, pressing his lips to mine as punishment. His tongue is warm, and his heavy strokes remind me exactly what that sinister tongue can do to other parts of my body.

It's not long until we arrive at his apartment, and he slowly pulls away, my body a trembling mess in complaint.

I grab his hand. "Can't we wait a little bit," I ask eagerly, wanting him to finish what he began.

"You shouldn't have been late," he chides as he steps out and circles the car to open my door.

My mouth is agape. *Is he saying no to me?*

He takes my hand and leads me to the elevator, where he inserts a key and then clicks the button for the penthouse. He stands behind me, his hands around my waist, holding me to him. He spreads kisses up my neck and pushes my hair out of the way. The doors open to reveal two women standing there. One is Angel, and the other I don't recognize.

"Mama," Crue says, still holding on to me.

My blood runs cold.

His mother reaches for me and pulls me out of Crue's grip until I'm following her—more like being dragged—into the kitchen.

"You're late," are the first words she says. And I

have the distinct impression this is the very person Crue gets his need for punctuality from.

She seems to have already cooked and is now putting the finishing touches on the food.

"I-I'm sorry," I stammer, unsure what else to say.

"Mama Monti loves things done on time," Angel explains, coming up to stand next to me. "So glad you could come. We only have a few days left, and Mama Monti has wanted to meet you all this time." And my cutting glare in Crue's direction reminds him of the fact I'm not at all comfortable with being ambushed like this.

"You shouldn't have left it for so long until I got to meet her." Mrs. Monti waves a wooden spoon with sauce on it in the general direction of Crue and me. And I'm unsure if she's mad with her son or both of us.

"I had to meet you. My son has said for a long time he plans to marry you. I'm glad to see him sticking to his word. And I am glad you are so beautiful, not that I expected less. I mean, my son has great taste. Takes after his mother," she says.

My blood freezes while that constricting feeling creeps up my chest. All I heard out of that was *marry me*.

"We aren't getting married," I tell her. And I give

everyone a hard look to remind them of that fact and that I have a say in this too.

She stops stirring the sauce and narrows her eyes at me. "No marriage?" She turns to Angel. "Did you know of this?"

"I—"

"Don't annoy Rya, Mother," Dominic says, entering the kitchen. "It's her first night with us." Dominic puts an arm around me and pulls me in. "We don't want to scare her off. Crue does a good job of that by himself."

"Remove your hands from her," Crue says darkly.

Dominic drops his arm as his mother and Angel carry plates to the table. I feel Crue approach before he circles my waist from behind.

"This is awkward. How dare you put me in this situation without warning," I quietly seethe at him. When he said we were going to celebrate my winning the case, I thought perhaps a fancy dinner and great sex. Not being bombarded with family. Not that I'm complaining about seeing Angel, but his mother that's an entirely different story.

"You think this situation is awkward? Is it any worse than your mother walking in while I held a gun over my hard cock?"

"That's not the same." I turn around so I can see

him. "I didn't know she was coming. You knew I was meeting your mother."

"Well, you can't meet my father because I killed him."

I huff out a breath as he pulls away and drags me with him to the table, where everyone is already seated. He pulls out a chair for me, and I sit. I note with surprise that some of the meals are vegetarian. I wasn't hungry until I sat in front of the food. With the excitement of the day, I haven't had the chance to eat. Crue hands me the platter of garlic bread, starts to plate up some pasta for me, and then does the same for himself.

It's strange to see Crue doing something so... human.

"Wine?" his mother offers.

I throw my hand up so quickly it draws everyone's attention as a nauseous swirl begins in my stomach. "I'll skip the wine, thank you."

Crue chuckles as he takes the wine from his mother and pours himself a glass instead. "Rya here had a little too much over the weekend."

"An Italian woman who doesn't drink wine is—"

"Mom." Dominic flattens her with a stare.

She perks right back up with a smile. "So, Rya, do you plan to move back home soon?"

Oh boy, are we in for a cracker of a night. I start to

eat my food and cover my mouth at his mother's question before I answer while tension ripples through the room, "No," I state, making it abundantly clear.

Her gaze cuts straight to Crue, and I feel the judgment there.

"How is work?" Angel asks me, trying to change the subject. "I see you won the Torrisi case. That's huge!"

"Do you plan to have kids one day?" Crue's mother interrupts with another question.

"Mother," Crue scolds.

"No," I answer, then take another defiant bite.

"You can't marry her," his mother announces.

This time, heat boils my blood. "I am *not* marrying him."

"Good." She nods her head.

"Rya," Crue says.

I put my fork down. "I have to use the restroom. Angel, could you show me where it is?"

I already know where the bathroom is, but she excuses herself anyway.

"Of course." She gets up, holding her belly as she does. We walk from the kitchen, and I hear them arguing in Italian. I know every word. I speak it fluently.

"Get me out of here," I beg, gripping her arm.

"I know she comes off gruff, but I promise she is a good woman. She's just emotional because she's getting her first grandbaby, and there's a lot of pressure on Crue right now from the families in Italy. Don't worry about what she has to say."

"I'm not. It's why I want to leave. It was just supposed to be sex," I tell her.

"And you're certain *he* knows that?" she asks, walking toward the elevator. She punches in a code, and the doors open.

"I have made it abundantly clear," I snap at her. When I see her wide eyes, I'm quick to apologize. "I'm sorry. I didn't mean—"

"It's okay. I'll give you a five-minute head start. But his phone will alert him the moment the elevator has been used. I'll try to buy you more time."

This time I give her an appreciative hug.

Because, fuck me, I fell for it again.

This back and forth between me and Crue.

This constant dance.

And I yet again find myself on the run.

CHAPTER 52
Crue

My phone beeps as Angel shuffles back into the room. She walks over and touches my shoulder. "The baby is kicking. Here, feel it." She reaches for my hand and places it on her belly. I sit there awkwardly and wait. "Oh, she must have stopped." She giggles before she returns to her seat and says, "Rya won't be long." And when she says it, her face reddens.

My phone beeps again, and this time when I check it, I see it's a notification from my elevator. I look up to see Angel nervously stuffing her face with food. And that's when I see Rya on my screen—she exits the elevator and walks to a waiting cab outside.

"Angel?"

"What? She's my friend."

"What happened?" my mother asks.

"You scared off my future wife, that's what," I growl at her.

"She won't marry you, that one. She wants the American dream of riches and work. She doesn't want what you want."

"You will accept her, Mother, or I'll cut you off as well." I push up from the chair and stride to the elevator, Dominic quickly following.

"Maybe this isn't so smart. She hasn't warmed up to the idea, and time is ticking."

"I don't want to marry anyone else but her," I tell him.

"I get it, I do. But—"

"There's no but, Dominic. If I can't have her, I will not marry *at all!*"

Dominic seems surprised by my outburst, and my mother blatantly interjects. "You will not cut down tradition all because of some little wannabe American."

"Watch the way you speak about her. You'll be taking orders from her soon enough."

My mother scoffs and crosses her arms. That younger spitfire version of herself always comes to the forefront. "That woman wants no part of our family name."

"Crue." It almost sounds as if Dominic is pleading, drawing my attention away from our mother. "Your decision affects us all."

My gaze narrows on him. "Do you think I don't know that? How much have I done for you all?"

My mother flinches at my tone.

Angel stays back, her hand on her stomach as she leans against the wall for support.

They might not realize the lengths I have gone to for them, but I will not let anyone dictate what it is I do, especially considering they've never been disappointed in the riches and lifestyle my contribution has provided.

"I *will* marry the Ricci woman!" I shout, determined. "Even if I have to cut off her legs so she can't run."

I hear Angel gasp as I leave the room.

I'm fucking furious that my family would dare turn against me or even defy my judgment.

CHAPTER 53

Rya

Everything in me wants to return to my place, but Crue knows where I live and how to get in. And right now, I need to stay away from those magic hands that make me think I need him. Or worse, that I want him and no one else.

Monica opens the door, looking relieved to see me.

"I—" She cuts me off by pulling me in for one of her hugs. I let her and stand there awkwardly. To be honest, I had to go somewhere he wouldn't know where to look and this was my only thought.

"I've been keeping my distance. I wanted to give you time. But I had faith that our friendship would prevail." She smiles, her hands still on me.

"This was a mistake," I say, turning to leave.

"Don't go, please." She grabs for me, and I step back.

"Don't touch me."

"Why are you here?" she asks.

"I'm trying to avoid someone."

"Crue," she says.

I eye her with suspicion. "Are you still spying on me?"

She shakes her head. "No, but I know he is here to collect you."

"To collect me?"

"I guess so. Everyone back home knows that you're his."

"I'm his?" I ask, confused.

"Yep." She nods. "I warned your father that you wouldn't just accept it, but what would I know?" She shrugs.

"I have to go."

"Stay. Please. He won't find you here."

I know she's right. But staying here gives the impression that I've forgiven her, and I don't forgive her for lying to me for that long. She had many opportunities to tell me the truth.

"I won't bother you. You can have the couch. I'm off to bed anyway." She holds open her door, and I look inside and wonder which one I'd rather face—her or Crue. I pick the lesser evil—her. She smiles at me and quickly closes the door behind me.

Her apartment hasn't changed in any way, but it all feels different now. I was here not even six weeks ago, eating takeout and drinking wine.

She walks to the closet where her spare blankets and pillows are stored. I look at the photographs around her place. Some with her family. Or her supposed family. I wonder how deep this lie ran about our friendship. I wonder if anything she told me was true.

"They're my real family if that's what you're wondering," she says as she dumps the blanket and pillow on her coffee table. She goes to pull on the couch that turns into a sofa bed, but I know too well it's outdated and has a trick to it.

"I'll help," I offer, then we heave it open until it clicks into place.

She brushes off her hands and puts the bedding on while I silently help her.

"I stopped taking money from your father, by the way."

Oh, goodie, this is the exact conversation I want tonight. "That's because we stopped being friends."

She sighs. "I didn't tell your father that part because I still consider you my friend."

"It seems like a lot of people struggle to take hints these days," I mumble.

She laughs. "Yeah, well... if you have Crue Monti on your ass, me trying to be your friend is the least of your concerns."

I stop pulling out the sheet, still baffled by how casually she mentions my father and Crue—two powerful men in my life that I deliberately stepped away from and purposefully kept her out of the loop on. And she fucking knew all along.

"Did you know Crue would be there that night... at my birthday?"

"No," she says flatly and stares at me. She's not lying. I can tell. She waits for me to hook my sheet over the corner on my side. "But I knew he'd be on his way soon enough. I had no idea he was already in town."

"He's been here for years, apparently."

She freezes at that.

"Shit spy you make if you didn't know that much."

"Shut up." She laughs as she throws a pillow at me. I catch it, still conflicted by how I should interact with her.

"Just because I'm staying here doesn't mean I forgive you."

"I've never known a Ricci to forgive." She rolls her eyes.

"You know my family well, then?"

"No, but my father knows yours. It's how this whole arrangement came about. My father owed him a favor, and I got dragged into the crossfire."

I certainly know how that feels. *What the fuck is it with these old men making promises that involve their daughters?* Like, shit, do things yourself.

We begin to pull up the blanket. "But, Rya, I want you to know it wasn't always about that. At the start, I almost hated you because of it. But then I realized you were just... well, normal."

I laugh at that. She knew my family name and still considered me normal. Perhaps I wasn't the only delusional one in this friendship.

"I know I can't be forgiven for lying to you, but I sure as hell can try to make up for it." She tosses down a pillow.

I sigh. I'd fought and ran away from too many demons tonight. "Monica, the last six weeks have been hell. Right now, I just can't."

She nods in understanding. "I know. I just wanted you to know that before you run out of here like a bat out of hell in the morning. You've always been so very good at that."

My eyebrows furrow as she locks the front door. "Good at what?"

"Running."

I huff out a breath, and she gestures—no malice intended—with her hands. "Outside of the courtroom, I mean." Those words don't make it any better.

"Good night, Rya," she adds before stepping into the hallway that leads to her room. And the way she says my name now feels different. No more secrets to hide behind.

My two worlds have collided.

Past and now.

CHAPTER 54

Rya

The next morning, I decide to walk from Monica's. I wander the bustling streets of New York, the city busy with life even in the early morning, and somehow, I manage to walk aimlessly until midday. I can't help but think about many questions and conclusions, most of them centered around Crue.

Right now, the most pressing thing is... *how I am going to get out of this marriage.*

And there is the small question of... *whether it would really be that bad if I didn't.*

I squash that idea pretty quickly, though.

There is all this pressure not only from him but also from everyone else. I hate him. But there is something there that I'm not willing to acknowledge. So I push the thought down further because I'm certain that's the issue causing the anxious swirls in my stomach.

When I look up from the sidewalk to my building entrance, I'm surprised that Mr. Luca is standing there and discussing something with my doorman.

"Miss Ricci, do you know this man?" the doorman asks.

"Yeah, he's my..." *Boss isn't the right word*, "... colleague. What are you doing here, Mr. Luca?"

He's holding flowers and a bottle of champagne. "Well, I didn't realize you would take a few days to cool off after the case, so I didn't have the chance to give you this in congratulations!" He offers me a bouquet of mixed flowers, and there's a distinct smell in there I don't like, and worse than that, I pale at the sight of the champagne. Yep, it's still too soon.

"How did you find my address?"

Mr. Luca suddenly dips his chin and clears his throat, seeming embarrassed. "Oh, sorry. It was in your employment file. To be honest, I wasn't sure if it was up to date since you filed that information like ten years ago."

I study him.

This is definitely weird and I can't help but furrow my brows.

"I just wanted to check in and see if you had time for dinner in celebration," Mr. Luca says.

I stand there awkwardly, shifting from one foot to the other, unsure as to whether he's asking me out for dinner for work or a date.

"I'm so sorry, Mr. Luca, but I have plans today. Perhaps some other time," I reply gently, not wanting to encourage him but also not wanting to burn any bridges at work.

And then there's Crue.

Agreeing to dinner with another man *for any reason* would be like setting them up for a death blow. I hate that I now take that into consideration.

"Oh, of course. No problem. Well, I hope you enjoy the flowers. And again, congratulations. The board is extremely proud of your accomplishments. And the Torrisi family were clearly grateful with the generous bonus they sent through."

"Bonus?" I ask.

He's already walking away when he nods in confirmation. "Yes. The accounting department is processing it today, so you should receive the payment in the next day or so."

Considering how scared Andreas looked the last time I saw him, I didn't think he would be offering me a bonus anytime soon.

"Thank you," I reply to Mr. Luca as he leaves.

The doorman watches him leave and then turns back to me. "He doesn't look like your usual type," he says with a low chuckle. This man has been here since before I moved into the building, and so curiosity gets the better of me.

"And what does my *usual type* look like?" I ask with a sly smirk.

"The type that's no good for you. My daughter went through the same phase." He rolls his eyes, and I can't help but laugh. He might not be wrong. Before Crue, I suppose the type of men I dated were, in comparison, quite mundane. Not that I ever saw them again.

Where I once considered Crue a season or even a bad-boy phase, I'm not so sure anymore. What I do know is that I don't like it when another man gives me flowers or champagne.

CHAPTER 55

Rya

He's here.

I just know he is.

Before I even step into my apartment, I can smell him. I walk in to find Crue on my couch, watching television. As soon as he notices me stepping into the room, he stands.

"Why were you gone all night?" Crue asks. "And who gave you those?" He eyes the flowers and champagne.

"I should have known the moment another male is on the scene, you'd smell it like a bloodhound."

His gaze turns dark and threatening. "*Who* gave those to you?"

"Why are you here?"

"Waiting for you. Please get dressed. We have plans today."

"Are you sure your mother would approve of that?"

"Do I look like a man who cares what his mother thinks?" Crue raises a brow, his gaze scanning over me and stopping at my ankle. "You're still wearing my anklet."

I realize that I forgot to remove it.

"It's coming off."

"Keep it on. For today at least."

"I need to shower." I turn toward my bedroom and yell over my shoulder, "You can show yourself out." When I get to my room, I undress before I turn the shower on and step in. I wash, then turn to rinse my face and find him watching me. "Why are you still here? Didn't I tell you to leave?"

"I told you I have plans with you today."

"What's so urgent?" I ask, rinsing myself off. When I step out, he hands me a soft, white fluffy towel. I wrap it around myself and catch it at the top, but he catches my waist as I try to pass him.

"Wear a dress today."

My nose scrunches up at the order in his voice, so defiant as ever I ask, "Why?"

His gaze drops to my anklet again. "So I can see that."

I shake my head at his request, and when I try to pull away again, he leans in and kisses me. This man steals my breath and any rational thought along with it. His lips touch the corner of my mouth, and he kisses me softly.

"I planned to do a lot of dirty things to you last night," he relays against my lips.

"Like?" I turn toward him. My body hungers for him. But fuck me. How long can I do this to myself? This back and forth. This to and fro. I literally went to the one place where I thought he couldn't find me last night to what? Fuck him again the next day. This makes no sense.

"For one, I wanted to slide my fingers up your leg because I know how much you love that." He does that movement right now, sliding his hand up my leg, leaving goose bumps in his fingers' wake. "Then I would get so close, and you would wiggle your hips so I'm touching where you want me." I do as he says. "Right there," he whispers, applying pressure before he slides a finger inside me. His thumb circles my clit as he kisses me again.

This time, I give him my all.

Because this man can kiss.

And he makes me forget about what we were even fighting about. I rip at his clothes as my towel flutters to the floor. His shirt comes undone, and I pull at his belt, undoing it, then I unzip him and pull his cock out. I waste no time before I wrap my arms around his neck, and he lifts me, knowing what I want. I twine my legs around his waist, gripping tight. I feel him there, and he smirks as he positions himself. I lean in and nip at his lip before I take it in my mouth and suck hard.

I freeze when I feel Crue entering me. He lowers me slowly, then pauses all together. "Princess?" he says, and I hear the question.

"Fuck me already, Crue."

"Of course," he says, and with a sinister smile, he lifts me up and ever so slowly lowers me back down, teasing me until I grip his shoulders and start moving faster.

"Are we needy today?" he taunts. "Have I not been making you feel fulfilled lately, princess?"

"Will you stop calling me that?" I thread my fingers through his hair, pulling it back to expose his neck to me. I lean in and suck, marking him as he has done to me many times, while I continue to glide up and down on his thick cock.

He feels so... damn... good.

"I can feel you tightening." His face tilts back

down to mine and he leans into my ear to quietly say, "Come for me, princess... all over my bare cock." I don't register all his words, but I hear the part where he told me to come. And I do. My head falls to his shoulder, and I clutch hold wherever I can. I hold on for dear life, but I don't need to because he has me, and he isn't letting go until I'm ready.

Crue continues to thrust, and I feel another orgasm building inside me. *How can he do that?* "There she is," he says as I come a second time and we finish together this time. He holds and moves back into the shower, turning the faucet on before putting me down and stepping back out. He walks to the sink, grabs a washcloth, and wipes himself clean while I stand there as the incredible feeling of hot water washes over me.

"Top two yet?" he asks.

"Possibly," I reply casually as I rewash myself.

"I'll make you admit I'm number one." Crue does up his pants and walks out.

I finish up in the bathroom, only to enter the bedroom to find he's already picked a dress from my closet and has it lying on the bed. It's a long white dress with pink flowers in a design on the fabric. I slip it on and put my hair in a bun before applying light makeup.

He's on his phone when I enter the living room, but he hangs up once I reach him.

"Ready?" he asks.

"Yes, as long as it's not another "parent" surprise." I use air quotes as I deliberately roll my eyes.

"That's impossible to do when you've already met my only living parent," he replies. "And besides, she leaves tomorrow."

"Angel too?"

"Yep. She leaves tomorrow as well." Crue looks me over. "Beautiful as always." He pulls me into him and holds tight.

"Heels or no heels?" I ask.

"Heels," he replies.

I grab a pair of shoes at the door before we leave.

Crue stays quiet when we're in the car. Occasionally, he kisses my hand as he grips it, our fingers intertwined. He's not usually the chatty type, but an ominous silence surrounds him for our entire trip.

The car slows, parks, and he gets out, rounding the car. I have goose bumps running up my arms because something feels off. He opens my door, and as I look up we are in front of an old building. His fingers remain tightly intertwined with mine as we approach the entrance. Crue pushes the large doors open, and I spot Angel immediately when he does. She meets my eyes and just as quickly glances away. When I assess the space I find a man is standing at the far end.

Is this a church?

No way.

It can't be. *Right?*

Angel and Dominic stand, and right next to them is Crue's mother, who does not look happy to be here.

"Uh, Crue?" Crue doesn't say a word as he leads me toward the unknown man, who, on closer inspection, is definitely a priest. "What is happening?" It takes me longer than it should to realize what's happening. When it finally registers, I try to tug Crue back, but we're already in front of the priest.

Finally, I can pull my hand free, and then I glare at Crue. "What are you doing?" I hiss.

"You told me not to ask you again," he says like it should be obvious. "So I won't." He turns to the priest and nods his head.

"Welcome," the priest says.

I place my hand on Crue's cheek, turn his head to get close, and growl, "I will *not* marry you. How many times do I have to tell you?" I pull away and take a step back.

"Rya—" He starts, but I put up my hand.

"Sex does *not* mean I will marry you. What don't you get about that?"

"I have to get married, Rya. I'd like it to be to you."

"You don't *have* to do anything," I tell him.

"Oh, but I do. *Please...*" he slowly approaches me and cups my cheeks, "... let it be you."

"I won't marry you, Crue."

"Well, this is fucking torture," I hear Dominic mutter, but I don't pay him any attention. Crue looks deep into my eyes, and the pleading look can only be described as desperate.

How is it possible this man could be desperate? He could have anyone he wants.

"This *has* to end," I say out loud. "I have entertained this too long." I shake my head. "I have to go."

Crue's hand shoots out and grabs my wrist, pulling me in close. That's when his nostrils flare, and the vein in his neck pulsates like it might explode. His high chin and protruding eyes tell me he is more than angry. He is furious!

But does he not realize that what he's done here is wrong on so many levels?

"I've played nice, and I've been patient," he seethes.

"You shot a man for touching me!" I scoff and hear the priest behind us splutter, but he covers it with a cough. "Is that what you consider nice or patient?" I try to loosen his grip on me but he smirks and lifts his hand to the back of my head, then leans his forehead against mine. "Yes, because any other woman who dared say no, I would have made her crawl down that fucking aisle if she had half the attitude you do." I try to push away, but he holds me tightly, and his eyes remain firmly on mine. "Marry me, or so help me God—"

Before he can say anything else, I reach for his waist and grab his gun.

"You won't use it," he says confidently.

"Yes, I damn well will," I reply, then shoot his leg. He releases his grip on me.

I drop the gun and then say, "Marry your fucking mother for all I care!" I scream at him before I run, as fast as my legs will fucking carry me.

Runaway bride and a fucking bullet wound in my leg.

Perfect!

Just fucking perfect!

"It's fine. She just nicked me," I say as my mother fusses around me while I am trying to brush her away.

"You are too kind to that woman. It's time to show her the real you," she demands, vengeance lacing her tone, and her eyes are flinty as all fuck.

"No. I won't force Rya to marry me."

"You kind of just tried," Angel points out. "And I knew this wouldn't work."

"Fuck! You really pissed her off," Dominic adds.

"Everyone shut the fuck up!" I yell, and the priest gasps. "Jesus Christ," I mutter under my breath.

Flashes of her beautiful, ruthless smile come to mind at the memory of her first asking me if I'd ever been shot. Then, the warning shot at the lamp beside my head in her apartment. I begin to laugh, a vexing delight bubbling from my stomach. I should have fucking known she would be the first and only to ever actually shoot me.

The others look at one another, their faces showing concern but also waiting for the inevitable explosion they know is coming.

Time is running out.

I only have a few months left until this contract needs to be signed, and here I am, bleeding all over a chapel floor where I was meant to marry my incredibly reluctant bride.

"Let's get you up," Dominic offers.

I push him away. "I can get the fuck up myself." Goddamn, this shit hurts.

But not as much as the pain and wrath I will rain down on her.

Retaliation, as she will find out, is a real bitch!

As I sit back in my leather office chair, I down the whisky while watching the blaze live on the news channel. Dominic checks on me like he's been doing all afternoon.

"Right on cue," he says to break the ice.

I turn up the volume, purposefully ignoring him.

"FIREFIGHTERS WERE on the scene immediately. But what's left of the Torrisi mansion..." The reporter turns to the burned-out shell. "Well, as you can see, there isn't much. It's said that the family had gathered only an hour before, continuing belated birthday celebrations for the head of the family, Andreas Torrisi, when something short-circuited in the home, setting it ablaze. Others suspect that with recent news and conflict around Matteo Torrisi's case, where he was found innocent, this might somehow be a retaliation to that decision. Once we know more, we will bring it to you."

I TURN THE TELEVISION OFF, satisfied by at least that much. The explosives we used in their home that night were intentionally placed to make it look like an accident. And my meeting was only a distraction for what was really at play.

A low tap comes on the door. "Boss? There's a delivery."

I nod at Dominic to let him in. The man strolls in with what looks like a white cake box.

I motion for my man to open the lid.

Dominic and I peer in simultaneously, and despite my mood, a cruel smile spreads on my lips. It's Francesca's head, quite literally on a silver platter.

"You played them against each other," Dominic says.

Little had they realized that their time would come to an end exactly as I expected it to.

Francesca had led me into their home hoping she would soon become heir once I told her of my plan. And Andreas had discovered the identity of the person who put out the hit on me and, as promised, delivered their head to me. I look over to the recent documents signed by Andreas Torrisi, granting me fifty-one percent of all profits of the whiskey business. And because there is no longer a known heir for the business, as the largest shareholder, it now belongs to me.

"This is a huge win today," Dominic says, but his voice grows quiet at my steely expression. I throw back my whiskey, furious.

It should feel like a win today.

But this doesn't get me any closer to fulfilling the contract I need and have fixed on for half my life.

"What are you going to do, Crue? She won't come back."

"You think I don't fucking know that?" I yell, throwing my empty glass across the room, the glass hitting the wall and breaking into a thousand pieces. A hot twang of pain floods my leg again. *Shit*. I split open the stitches.

"I'm going to do what I always do. I'll fix this mess up."

H ow dare he? Who the fuck does he think he is? Taking me to a church and hoping I would marry him.

No is a simple word.

So what part of that word does a highly intelligent man like Crue not under-fucking-stand. I have told him several times I do *not* want to get married. I don't intend to *ever* get married. So what the fuck kind of stunt was that shit back there? I rip at my hair. This man is making me crazy? The frustration has boiled over into insane exasperation. I am beside myself and going out of my damn mind.

This is it.

The final straw.

Absolutely no more.

My phone pings, and I rip it out of my pocket, half expecting it to be an email from the dumbass, and for once, I might reply and give him a piece of mind.

Instead, it's a text message from Mr. Luca.

> Mr. Luca: Turn to the news right now!

MY EYEBROWS SCRUNCH IN CONFUSION. Not any particular channel, just any old news? I decide to turn on the television before asking for further instructions as to what channel, but there's no need. My jaw drops in shock because I know exactly whose mansion is in flames on my screen and I raise a brow while listening.

"IN RECENT REPORTS, it's thought that the fire may be linked to criminal activity associated with the most recent case involving Matteo Torrisi. It's no secret that his father was killed a little over a year ago in a shooting with a rival gang. Now the question remains... Is this once again gang-related, or has the opposing family in *the recent court decision taken matters into their own hands? Stay tuned as we investigate further."*

"WHAT THE FUCK?" I say as I put my hand over my mouth. *What the actual fuck?* Memories of our visit there and the calculated flow of Crue's movements flood me. *He definitely had something to do with this.*

My phone begins to ring, and I answer.

"Have you seen it?" Mr. Luca asks.

"I'm watching it now."

"What happened?"

"How should I know? This is the first time I've seen or heard about it."

"This isn't good. Maybe you should lie low for a little while longer."

"Lie low? What do you mean? I was only taking a few days off after my case," I argue.

"I know. But this is bad and could possibly reflect back on us. Let the board handle it."

"Handle it? But it's my client."

"*Was* your client," he corrects.

"You can't tell me what to do," I say.

"No, but it's called good judgment, Rya. Trust me. Think rationally. Even if it's just a week until the media settles."

I sigh. My phone pings. "I'll take it under consideration. I have to go. I have another call coming through," I lie.

I hang up on him mid-sentence, and my eyes widen at the screen. And the many zeros that have just hit my bank account. Way too many zeros. Too generous for a bonus. Like I can retire and buy this building, if not the street, and retire as well.

What the fuck is happening?

Crue.

That's what happened.

That's what seems to always be the common denominator.

But considering only a few hours ago, I shot him in the leg, I can't exactly ask him for answers.

Assuming he's still alive, that is.

I sit across from Angel.

I'm pissed off.

But I am trying to be as reasonable as I can in hopes that I don't seriously stress a woman who's about to give birth at any moment.

"He's fine, just in case you wanted to know," Angel offers as she picks at her fries. We're having Five Guys again. This time, it's just the two of us—and two bodyguards.

"I didn't," I reply. "How did you think I would agree to something like that?" I try to watch my accusatory tone.

"I told him you wouldn't go for it. Trust me, I made the point loud and clear. But you know what he's like."

I breathe out a frustrated sigh. My nails click against the table in clear agitation, not at her but at this situation I find myself in now.

"I'm pretty sure he's in love with you," she says softly.

A cruel laugh creeps from my throat, and she stares at me as if I'm half-crazed. "The only thing Crue Monti cares about is power and where he can get more of it."

She winces at my words. "The guy's an ass. I am not going to defend him. But I'm also going to call you out on your shit as well." She points an accusative finger at me. "Sex? That's all you thought it was? Please. I have stood in the room with you two on more than one occasion. You can't keep your eyes off each other. You are both like magnets drawn to each other with an insatiable need. He's always mentioned you since you met as teenagers. You might've forgotten about him, but he most certainly did *not* forget about you.

"I've known Crue for almost fifteen years now, and granted, I still don't like him much." She pops a fry in her mouth. "But he's the uncle of my daughter. And he was becoming different with you around. Softer even."

I want to laugh at the thought of Crue as anything

less than cruel. But what right did I have? She's known him longer than I have. And me? Well, I was nothing but a season. And I sure as hell made sure of that.

"If you're trying to convince me to rekindle things with him, it's not going to work. I won't step back into that world."

"Ironic, wouldn't you say, considering you became a criminal lawyer? I don't think you've stepped that far away from our world at all."

"Ouch." Angel sure as hell isn't pulling any punches tonight. Not that I care—we never did with each other—but it jumbles my thoughts around the situation. Had I, at some point, been out of place? No. My nails have turned into a rapid drumming on the table now.

No.

He's a killer.

A criminal.

An obsessed stalker.

Crue Monti is an absolute no-go zone. Hot as fuck or not.

"And besides, I don't think you have to worry about him trying anything with you anymore. He's already left for the airport. He's going back home."

My tapping on the table stops. "For real?" And instantly, there are mixed feelings in my stomach of sweet relief and something else I refuse to acknowledge. "Good. Finally." I throw my hands up in celebration. "Now I can continue with my life like none of this ever happened." I didn't expect him to go running after I shot him. I supposed that was a good enough reason for a normal person to leave, but this is Crue we're talking about. Somehow I have ended up looking like the crazy person in this situation?

Angel seems sad when she picks at her half-eaten burger. "We leave tomorrow," she adds, her voice breaking a little as she sniffs.

I grimace. "I'll come and visit."

"You've been saying that for almost fifteen years now, bitch."

An exhausted laugh escapes me. "Right back at you. But I know... I will try harder."

"Especially now that you have a goddaughter to meet soon." She looks down at her stomach. "One who has an appetite for America's greatest burger chain, apparently." She chuckles and sobers again.

"I'm sorry to ask, but do you know anything about the Torrisi mansion going up in flames?" I question.

She shakes her head. "Nope. Even Dominic's staying quiet about that one. But I have no doubt of Crue's involvement. Why? Does it look bad because you were defending one of them?"

I shrug. "Kind of. There's another thing, though..." I glance around to ensure no one is paying us attention, and then I show her my bank balance. It's not like I'm not used to money. But I always made a point—besides my father paying for my education—to earn everything my way while trying to become as independent as possible.

And this type of money...

... it is blood money.

It reeks of it.

Angel looks from my phone and back to me. I have forgotten she's used to this amount of money, so I change the screen to the balance in there only one day ago.

"Oh, wow, that's a big difference. You were living off that before?" she asks suspiciously.

I give her an unimpressed look.

"Sorry." She winces.

By standard wages, I earn a fuck-ton more than most. But this is old money. Money, I've been advised, is a generous bonus. But to me, it smells a lot like Crue Monti. And I don't want his charity. In fact, I don't want anything else from him again.

"Couldn't you open your own firm with money like that?" she asks around a mouthful of her burger.

That hadn't crossed my mind. "Maybe." I tuck my phone away. "So, when do you leave tomorrow?"

She rolls her eyes. "Early. Apparently, we have to go to the family home for some big announcement."

"Sounds serious."

"It usually is. But it could just be because Crue is returning."

My nail tapping resumes at the mention of him returning to Italy.

She watches me cautiously. "Are you sure you're okay?"

I laugh. "No. This motherfucker is getting a bill for *all* my therapy."

She laughs, holding her belly.

"At least I can leave knowing you're okay," she says.

"You know me, I always get back on my feet. There's no way I'm letting any man get the best of me."

She lifts her thick shake to my soda water in cheers. "To all the men who should go fuck themselves."

I laugh. At least she was lucky. From what I've seen between her and Dominic, they are made for each other. Despite the name and his family, he treats her like a gift from God, and I have no doubt this little bundle of joy is going to be spoiled all the same.

"Can we also just talk about how you shot Crue?" she whispers so the guards don't hear us and then takes a huge bite of her burger. "You are one crazy bitch." She places the burger down and then applauds while she chews.

All I can do is smirk.

CHAPTER 59

Crue

"What did you expect?" my mother says, sitting across from me on the plane.

"Mother."

"No, Crue, what *did you expect*, really?"

I grind my teeth and remember to not kill my own fucking mother.

She needs to live.

But then again, what for?

"Don't give me that look, boy. Those businesses have been in the Monti family for six generations, and I will *not* let you be the first generation where it falls. You *will* marry before you turn thirty-four."

"I know this."

"Then get over yourself and figure it out."

"Why do you think I'm on a private jet back to Italy, *Mother*?"

"Because all your years in New York are for naught, and you're returning needing a bride in less than three months. That's why. You've left it too long."

I grit my teeth. I had forced myself to stay away from Rya for that long, vowing I would give her freedom until she turned thirty. But now, for the first time ever, I wasn't so sure about the card I played.

I thought... *Well, frankly, I don't know what I thought.*

Any woman would be blessed to have been looked upon by me twice. Let alone an offer of marriage for convenience. But it was more than that with Rya. I rub my leg. Well, I sure as shit was mistaken to think it was more than that.

There's nothing more abundantly clear than your bride shooting you so she can escape and run out of the chapel.

"The families are going to be in such a fuss when you come back unmarried. Had your father been here, he wouldn't have let any of this happen."

"For fuck's sake, Mother," I say, standing and pulling out my gun. Her mouth snaps shut. "Fuck!" I scream, pissed off that I pulled my gun on my own mother. "I told you not to mention him in front of me. Or Rya, for that matter. Do we understand one another?"

A scowl mars her expression as she pouts.

Had my father been here? For fuck's sake!

There's no point in telling her about that little hit he had once put out on her because I cleaned it up before she'd ever been the wiser. As I always did. As was my responsibility.

Like now.

I had to marry.

And I would find a wife.

My jaw grinds as I take a seat. "And besides, I've increased the family's profits by thirty percent since being in New York. I doubt they can complain about that."

She picks up the romance novel she was reading and looks it over. She's good at that. Looking down her nose at me to have the last word. "They will complain, and you know it. It's not enough. This is *tradition*, and tradition is everything to the families."

"Maybe I'll return and kill them all. I've become good at wiping out families lately."

"Watch your mouth," she hisses.

I roll my eyes and press the tip of the gun to my own head as I lean back in the seat. *Kill me now.* I might not make it through this flight with my mother's tongue lashing me the entire way.

But the truth is, I have already started putting a plan into action. I am going back to Italy out of necessity. There's a little package I need to collect to end this marriage discussion once and for all.

CHAPTER 60
Rya

Four weeks crawl by and I am suffocating.

I think about him way too often for my liking.

I managed to change the locks on my apartment in hopes that he wouldn't be able to break in again while secretly missing him.

It's a hard pill to swallow—to want someone but also to not want them at all. To come to the realization that he'd inserted himself so deeply into my life that I now feel lost without his overbearing presence.

What my life would be like with him is not something I will willingly choose.

So why would I make an exception for him?

I shouldn't and wouldn't.

Angel let me know she had the baby and sent me

photographs. I sent her flowers and gifts. Weeks go by, and I hardly hear from her, but that's to be expected, considering Angel's a new mother.

I returned to work two weeks ago and accepted my new role, but it doesn't feel as rewarding as I thought it would.

"We're getting you out of your slump and going to Italy," my mother says as I sit across from her in my kitchen, having a cup of tea.

"I can't just up and leave." It seems strange that my mother wants to return there since she'd sworn she never would. Sure, she mentioned it like a month ago, but I'd already told her no.

"Yes, you can. You've been playing good girl and lying low, and all you can show for it is what? An excessive time spent at the yoga studio?" She points to my baggy sweatshirt. I have, in fact, only just returned from my third hot yoga session of the day.

"Doctors advise it's healthy."

"There's nothing healthy about a woman pushing down her feelings and covering her workaholism with yoga pants."

I hate how perceptive my mother is with her small acknowledgment that I haven't been the same since the day Crue left. I don't like to admit the unsettling feeling his absence has left within my world.

"I don't have plans to go."

"Didn't you say your friend had a baby? Be a good friend and go visit the girl. I bet she would love that. New mothers are flustered, and time with familiar, trusted people is good for them. It's tiring being a mother." I control myself from reminding her that she was hardly a 'good' mother.

"I'll think about it."

"Don't think too hard. I booked a flight for us in two days."

"What?" I screech.

"I might not be a good mother, but I know when a woman needs an escape. Maybe a rendezvous with another man... no?"

A nauseous swirl stirs in my stomach. That doesn't sit well with me, either. Because in my dreams and fantasies, there's only one pair of hands I imagine touching me.

The doorbell buzzes.

My mother and I look at one another. My first thought is, *what if it's Crue?* But I know better than that. He would never buzz the door. That man would waltz on in as if he owned the damn place.

I stand and answer the door to a courier.

"Delivery for Miss Ricci," the man says, holding two boxes. "You need to sign for them."

My eyebrows knit in confusion. I don't remember ordering anything, even on the nights when I drank a whole bottle of wine to myself. I sign for the boxes, then take them inside. Grabbing a knife, I cut open the first box and shift the packing material to one side to reveal something red underneath.

Red leather and red lace.

Oh shit.

I forgot all about this.

My mother looks over and whistles appreciatively.

I didn't really think he would send it to me, but here I am, holding the most expensive thing I own.

Wow.

I find a note at the bottom.

> *Dear Rya*
> *I have requested Dawson send these your way. Even though you are a bitch, I still respect your body. And in doing so, I hate you.*
> *I want you to know that.*
> *I hate you.*
> *But I also want to fuck you again.*
> *In these outfits.*

But I can't and I won't.
Because I'm getting married.
And that wouldn't be very husband-like
of me, would it?
Do not throw this out.
Do not reply.
The man you fucked over and shot.

I SCRUNCH my nose up at the note.

And I don't want to try the lingerie on anymore.

He's getting married.

That was fast.

What's it been, like, a four weeks?

Fuck him.

I inhale a shaky breath and turn to my mother, who pretends she's busy looking elsewhere but most likely has read the note and knows everything.

"You know what? Let's go on that girls' trip," I all but seethe. *Fuck him.* Hot yoga and wine are not going to help me get over this unbearable asshole, and maybe taking my first holiday from work would be good for the soul.

SITTING across from my mother on a plane to Italy was not exactly what I had planned. I didn't end up telling Angel I was coming because I didn't want to risk her mentioning to Crue that I would be there. I don't want him to know I'm coming back home. I'm not going there to see him, so it's only fair he doesn't find out. But in saying that, I have a feeling nothing gets by him, and he will, without a doubt, figure out that I'm back.

My father and stepmother are waiting for me. As soon as I leave the airport, my father, despite being a ruthless man, has a kind smile when it's directed at one of his children. His arms wrap around me immediately, and my stepmother, Sharon, offers me a small wave.

"Where is Honey?" I ask them.

"She's going to meet us for dinner. I figured you would be down for a good meal," my father says.

I turn to find my mother, who is already in the arms of another man. Who, I might add, she never told me she was here to see.

"I'll see you later, sweetie." My mother waves and gets into a car with said man.

"Hasn't changed, I see," my father comments. "But I'm thankful she got you here. Your sister has been dying to see you." I technically haven't seen my sister since I left, but I have spoken to her many times on the phone and even FaceTime.

In her early teens, she went through a phase where she was boy-crazed. I remember my father calling and asking me to talk some sense into her because I wasn't the same at her age. But Honey and I couldn't be more opposite. She's bubbly, sweet, and she always talks to people with kindness.

As she grew older, our communication dwindled a little bit more each year. She was always happy with the fact that one day, she would be married and have children. It's the romantic in her where I have done everything humanly possible to run far away from that idea and life.

"I'm excited to see her as well. I do have to see a friend tomorrow who had a baby recently."

"Oh, that's lovely." My father puts an arm around me as we walk to his car, where his driver takes my bags as we climb in.

"You should tell her," my stepmother says.

"Tell me what?"

"Your sister has had a lot going on lately," my father says.

"Okay."

"I just hope you can cheer her up," he adds, looking at Sharon, who shakes her head.

Well, that was weird.

But being cryptic is definitely my father's thing.

We pull up at the restaurant, and I brush my hands down my trousers. I should have probably asked to go home and shower first and do my makeup. I look like I haven't slept for hours, which I didn't, and I'm still wearing the sweats I wore on the plane. My hair is up in a messy bun, and my face is bare.

My father places his hand on my back as he tells me about a new business he has opened. As soon as we enter, I hear my father say Honey's name.

When I look up, I stop dead in my tracks.

Sitting next to her is Crue.

He's whispering something in her ear, and she's smiling and giggling at him. Her eyes find mine, and she stills. Her lips pinch to a flat line before she stands.

And that's when I see it.

A fucking massive engagement ring on her finger.

I look at Crue to see him eyeing me with venom.

"It's okay, dear, just breathe," my stepmother says. "It will all be over soon."

I don't want to breathe.

For fuck's sake, I want to knock myself out and

pretend I didn't just walk in on this... this nightmare playing out in front of me.

Maybe it's a joke.

Maybe she's engaged to someone else and not *him*.

I turn my gaze back to Honey, her chestnut-colored hair curled and framing her face. Her eyes, which are the same as mine, stare back at me. Where mine are more than likely dead, hers are vibrant and full of life.

It takes both of us a moment to move. And when we do, I gather myself and walk around to where Honey's now standing. Ignoring *him*, I reach for Honey and pull her in for a one-armed hug while she puts both arms around me.

"I'm sorry I didn't tell you. I know you've been busy with the promotion, and I didn't want to take that moment away from you," she whispers.

Honey becoming engaged is no issue at all for me.

But the certain someone who is the intended groom, however...

Do I even have the right to be angry at anyone?

I mean, I shot the asshole to get him away from me.

And here he is.

Sitting with a smug look on his face.

Like he's won.

Pulling back, I smile at Honey and ignore Crue as I sit at the opposite end of the table. My father orders for me, already knowing what I like, then orders for the rest of the table.

When it goes quiet, Honey turns to me. "How's life? I've missed you so much."

"It's good. Busy with work," I tell her, keeping my answers short.

"Anyone new in your life?" she asks, and I see him twitch.

"I..."

"What about that guy you told me about last week? What was his name?" my father interrupts.

"Are you engaged?" I ask her, ignoring my father's questions. When, really, I was telling him about Mr. Luca and my discussion around having a short trip to Italy since I hadn't had a vacation since I started working at the firm. And I think he knew that.

The table falls silent. And Crue picks up his glass of wine, taking a sip.

"Yes," Honey says.

"To?" I ask. "I would love to meet the man who has that honor," I say a little louder.

"It's Crue," she says, looking to her left, where he's not paying us any attention.

"Oh, wonderful. I brought a present for you.

Though I didn't know at the time who your fiancé was, it will be the best honeymoon gift. It's red and lacy, perfect to wear to treat your husband."

His head spins, his gaze burning into me.

I smile gracefully at him and hold up my glass. "Congrats, Crue. You're finally getting what you want. A Ricci girl."

"Rya," my father warns.

"What? You know it's what he's wanted all along."

Crue stays silent, but I still feel his gaze firmly on me.

"If you will excuse me, I have to use the ladies' room." I push out of my seat and stroll to the restroom. As soon as the door closes behind me, I turn the faucet on and splash my face with water to help overcome all these mixed feelings I am having.

Fuck. What is happening?

CHAPTER 61

"I'll be a minute," I tell Honey, who offers me one of her sweet smiles, so innocent compared to her sister.

That mother fucking hell-raiser.

I walk straight into the ladies' room to find Rya splashing her face with water. She turns toward me, water dripping from her chin.

Even looking exhausted after a long flight, she's still the most beautiful woman I have ever seen.

"Get out," she says tiredly and turns away, reaching for a paper towel and drying her face while I stand there.

"You haven't asked how my leg is." I step closer and watch her tense up.

"I don't care."

"You haven't asked if I've fucked your sister yet." She shudders at my words.

"Are you really this deranged? This is a new low, even for you," Rya seethes.

"You haven't asked if I've stroked myself thinking of you every night since you left me in that chapel."

Rya's head whips around to face me. She points her finger at me and gets right in my face. "How. Dare. You. If you think for even a second that I would condone you cheating on or hurting my sister, you are very much mistaken."

"It's you who's hurting her because we both know which sister I would have picked."

"You tried to *force* me to marry you. Are you fucking kidding me? I knew there were a few screws loose up there, but come on. When did you think that would ever work?"

"I thought..." I'm at a loss for words.

She leans back and crosses her arms over her chest expectantly.

"I thought..." I can't seem to say the words I so desperately need to come to me.

As if she can almost hear the end of that sentence, she says, "You thought wrong, Crue. But how dare you use my fucking sister in the process. Do you realize how sick that is, how fucking perverted."

I grab her wrist, so infuriated that I want to break every bone in her body. But I also want to steal her away so no one else can touch her. The last five weeks have been a living hell without her. I don't know when it happened, but this fiery vixen is all I can think about, even when my engagement ring is on her damn sister's finger.

"I have thought about you every fucking night since I left America. I didn't force this hand. You did."

"By suggesting you marry my sister instead?" She scoffs out a deranged laugh.

"I wanted *you*. It's always been *you*," I seethe as I press my face close to hers.

Hot and insufferable.

Devastatingly beautiful.

Overwhelmingly impossible.

I want to reach out to this woman out of habit, but I use a restraint that I never knew I had to not claim what I know is one hundred percent mine.

Now Rya steps closer, coming nose-to-nose.

She's too close.

Too tempting.

Her voice is full of venom as she speaks, "You were something to pass the time," she says cruelly. "And here in Italy, who knows, maybe I'll find another victim to pass the time with."

"You will *not* be sleeping with anyone else." My grip tightens on her wrist enough to leave bruises. But how else do I get through to this stubborn woman?

"You don't own me." She shoves past me.

I'm about to snap and shoot every single person in this restaurant.

My rage is a burning inferno.

This woman is insufferable. Intolerable. And fucking *mine*.

I try to casually walk out behind her, but it's obvious how furious she is, and I'm probably a toxic dark cloud behind her.

"I have to go. I'm meeting someone. But I'll come by the house tomorrow. Are you fine with my things?" Rya says to her father.

He nods gravely.

"You're leaving already?" Honey jumps out of her seat and looks between me and Rya. "Is everything okay?" she whispers as if to not draw attention.

Honey's a well-trained woman. Completely opposite to this seething harpy across from me who has *way* too much attitude.

"Everything's fine," we both grit out at the same time as our gazes connect again.

"Actually, I think your fiancé is a complete dickhead."

"Rya!" Mr. Ricci snaps.

I raise my hand to him. "That's rich coming from the spoiled little runaway lawyer who is so ridiculously good at winning cases but so completely dense when it comes to her own duties."

"Duties?" she scoffs. "Why, because I refuse to spit out a baby and greet you with your slippers and a cigar every day you walk through the fucking door like a good housewife?"

We're both leaning over the table, yelling.

My gaze flicks around the room, everyone quickly averting their attention. This fucking woman has made me completely lose my composure.

But then her eyes fall to Honey.

Honey seems to shrink back.

When I reach out to her, she steps out of reach. It's a surprise that this good girl has a sliver of the backbone of her sister. What is it with these Ricci women? I've killed for less than this.

"Honey, let me explain," Rya begins.

"No. I think that's enough for one day," she says, sounding diplomatic, and looks at her father for approval. "I think that's enough of a show for everyone, isn't it?" But quietly, she turns to me. "It was never me you wanted, was it?"

Honey looks at me pointedly. And I don't know

what it is that she expects to see. Mercy? Comfort? She will see neither of those traits.

"I am contracted to have a Ricci bride, and I *will* have one," is all I say.

"You are such a *pig*!" A glass of water splashes my face from Rya's direction. She is *all rage* now. Even Honey knows better than to get in the middle as she steps back. Rya, however is vicious and hateful. And, fuck, those eyes of hers are shining with rage. I want to grab her and pin her against this table. This woman provokes every need in me, even in a situation like this.

My men step forward, but I raise my hand for them to stay out of it. Could I really reprimand Rya publicly in the same way I would others? If I did, she'd be dead.

"I'm sorry for my daughters," Mr. Ricci begins. "It's a very confusing situation."

"I think it's time we left," Honey says, quickly gathering her things.

"Honey, can we talk?" Rya stretches her hand out to her sister.

"No," Honey says with a tight smile. "Not today."

Honey's gaze is firm. A Ricci woman through and through. She's not the one I want, but she's the one I will be married to.

I lock gazes with the spitfire across from me. Her

caramel hair is coming loose from her bun and she looks like she's about to combust into flames.

"Maybe I should have aimed higher when I shot you."

"Maybe you should have just married me instead."

"Fuck off, Crue!" Rya flips me off and storms out.

Mr. Ricci sits there speechless. His wife blanched pale about two minutes ago.

"My daughter has always been very vocal," he finally says.

"Doesn't make for a good wife," I reprimand.

But my God, the only woman I want to be my wife is the one who lacks all of the qualities I am looking for in a plaint wife.

Rya being here changes nothing.

In two weeks, I *will* be married.

CHAPTER 62
Rya

I wasn't meeting anyone.

As quickly as possible, I went to the nearest hotel, jumped into the shower, and crawled into bed naked.

I should have brought my bag, but I hadn't planned to run away from my family.

I knew I couldn't sit there a second longer.

I need to sleep.

Maybe tomorrow, I'll be better prepared to deal with it.

I expected Crue to be marrying someone else, but I didn't expect it would *be my sister.*

I try to call her once, but it goes straight to voicemail.

So, out of respect, I will give her a day before I show up at my father's house.

"So it turned into a screaming match in a local restaurant?" Angel sits breastfeeding Alessia, looking at me dumbfounded. Then her worried gaze moves to Dominic.

"Yeah, basically," I say, defeated.

She whistles. "You two have absolutely lost your fucking minds."

"What? I'm not the psycho who came back to put a ring on my sister's finger and plan on marrying her in *two weeks*!" I immediately apologize for raising my voice as Alessia stirs.

We sit in Dominic and Angel's mansion—the couple having settled into family life. Dominic lounges next to Angel, his hand helping to cradle the baby, as if he wants to be a part of everything.

I find it strange to watch them. Angel is married with a kid now. The exact things I have been running away from my entire life. I wonder if my father and mother shared a moment like this. Whether they were the vision of doting parents. Or if my mother was out flaunting her newfound money and lifestyle the week after I was born.

"Yeah, we only received our wedding invitation today," Angel says as she nudges Dominic to hand it over. He blows out a low, begrudging breath as he holds it to me. And there, in writing, it states the time and date of Miss Honey Ricci being married to Mr. Crue Monti.

"Well, shit! Looks like he's willing to make a big deal of *their* wedding, whereas all I got was a forced attempt. We might as well have gone to Vegas and had Elvis marry us," I say bitterly as I hand the elegant invitation back to Dominic.

"Actually, he did consider that for you," Dominic says quietly.

Angel seems to encourage him. I can always see his reluctance when speaking about his brother because, amongst Crue's flaws, he was not opposed to killing family members if he felt wronged by them.

"Would you want a big wedding like this?" he asks.

"Fuck no."

He looks at me as if that is answer enough. "He wanted to keep it intimate and small. Where he didn't have to bring you back to Italy in front of the families because he knew you would blow a gasket."

"Well..." I hesitate. "I'm pretty sure when I made it

abundantly clear I *don't* want to marry, it should've stopped there."

"But he has to, Rya. He gave you as much time as he could."

"What is that supposed to mean?"

Angel flicks another quick glance at Dominic, and he sighs. "Shit, woman, you're really going to get me killed."

She rolls her eyes and speaks on his behalf, "He promised not to go near you until you turned thirty. He thought that would give you enough 'freedom' before he imposed on your life."

"Imposed?"

"He was always coming for you," Angel says as she stands and approaches me. I'm gobsmacked. I hate the knowledge that this was all contracted and planned without my consent.

"Here." She hands Alessia to me.

"Oh no... I'm not good with kids."

She huffs and plops the most fragile parcel in my arms. "Just because your mother wasn't and probably still isn't a good mother doesn't mean the same for you, Rya."

A twist forms in my stomach. I had never even imagined myself as a mother. I'm not like Honey or her mother. I didn't have that maternal instinct inside of me. But looking down at Alessia, as her godmother, I know I would do anything for this beautiful child. I pull back a corner of her blanket, marveling at how tiny she is. How fragile she seems.

I can feel Angel judging me before she says, "Do you think this is all because you're running away from what you think marriage and kids look like?"

I scoff. "I'm running away because he is a mafia boss who kills for sport. Or am I the only one who keeps remembering that part of his life?"

"You knew that before you slept with him... and during... and even now. Yet here we are, still talking about him."

"Because he is trying to marry my sister," I remind her.

Her expression turns sad. Pitying even.

"What is that look for?" I ask.

"I just wonder if you'll spend your entire life running."

"Excuse me?"

"Whether it's running away from Crue or some other man. Do you want to die alone?"

"Wow," I say, blinking rapidly. I was *not* expecting this type of pep talk.

"How long are you going to run? From this." She waves around the house. "Because it's not all bad. Sure, the work is a bit sketchy, and it can sometimes be risky. But isn't that why you love being a lawyer? The risk. The thrill. The lines that are blurred. The freedom that it offers you in being able to do whatever you want. Being Crue's wife, you would be one of the most recognized women both here and in New York in name alone. What are you actually after? Honey and Crue aside."

I blanch at her. *What the fuck am I supposed to say to that?*

At my silence, she continues, "Think about it. Would you have let him go if you weren't told that you had to marry Crue? Because we know he sure as hell doesn't want to let you go. Families and contracts aside, I think Crue's an asshole." Dominic shifts awkwardly beside her as if she's just spoken some horrific form of blasphemy. "But I also think he's as stubborn as you, and he's honestly probably the only man in the world who can handle your shit."

"My shit?" I ask, wounded.

"You eat men alive in the courtroom," she states. "You might lie to everyone else, but you can't lie to yourself forever. Maybe Crue is the only man who has ever been able to handle you. Are you sure you're willing to let that slip away because of some technicalities in a stupid contract?"

"He's a criminal."

"And you are the daughter of one. It's not that part that upsets you. So try to use something that makes sense as an excuse next time."

Well, fuck.

CHAPTER 63
Rya

My mind spins at Angel's insinuations.

The car jolts beneath me as I sit in the back seat. Driving up to my family home which I haven't visited in fourteen years feels nostalgic.

In so many ways, it hasn't changed.

But I have.

It's a mess. All of it. And now, I have to explain the entire situation to Honey, and my stomach drops at the thought. I hate that these circumstances are overshadowing our reunion. But I suppose I can count on Crue to fuck even this up.

I sigh. I'm tired. I have been blaming all of this on Crue alone. But didn't I have a hand in this as well? I say I hate him. And I'm certain of that much, but there's more to it than that. The small moments on the couch and watching television. The phenomenal sex. *Him*. Entitled. Possessive and all-consuming. As irrational as our time together was, I can't deny what Angel called me out on. It had been thrilling. It had woken me from my stupor.

I don't think I want to die alone, but I don't necessarily care if I do, either. But her insinuation of me running away was the eye-opener because hadn't Monica said something similar? I never ran away from anyone or anything in court. I would always take everything head-on. So why is it different when it comes to Crue?

I hate that this man still consumes my thoughts even when I know we're done.

We stop at the end of the gravel driveway, and the horse ranch that Honey had built for her fifth birthday is in the distance. She'd always been the princess, not me.

I find myself starting to battle with something. The familiar driveaway and perfectly lined trees. The mansion where I grew up. But it isn't the only one we own. We have numerous vacation homes. My favorite is the lake house, which is only two hours from here.

My eyebrows furrow at the commotion as multiple people usher in an array of white roses. At the front of the group is Sharon, who is assigning their locations.

When she spots me, she waves. I give her a little wave back but still keep my distance in case she tries to hug me again.

"What's all this for?" I ask, peering into the house that, despite all the commotion, doesn't look like it has changed a bit.

"The engagement party tomorrow night."

"Wow. That happened quickly. I'm surprised the Montis aren't hosting at their place." *Considering how controlling Crue is*, I think.

"Oh, they will be. Ours is tomorrow night, and they are having one at theirs on Saturday evening."

I roll my eyes. Of course. Because what's more lavish than two engagement parties on the same weekend? "Where's Honey?"

At this, Sharon's expression changes. She licks her lips nervously. "It might not be my place to say, but you need to sort this out before they're married. Honey looks up to you. You've put her in a really difficult position."

"I've put her in this position?" I say incredulously.

"There she is," my father calls out as he walks over to hug me. My stepmother immediately continues to direct the staff. "About yesterday..." he begins.

"Papa, not now. I want to talk to Honey about it first."

His jaw tics. He's probably on edge. The spectacle that was Crue and me at the restaurant would be going down a treat right now, and there would be a lot he would have to answer for. But he is still my father.

"She's in the kitchen. Come find me once you're done."

"Thanks, Papa." I offer him a quick squeeze before I enter the house. Besides the décor that changes seasonally, it's all the same. Memories of the old home during much simpler days flood my mind.

Honey's light laugh flutters through the air while a pang of guilt twists in my stomach. Who is making her laugh like that? Is it Crue? Does he make her laugh because of all the provocative things he might say to her, like he did with me? A pang of jealousy and remorse stirs in my stomach, but I push it back down.

I brace myself. And when I turn the corner into the white marble kitchen with floor-to-ceiling windows offering a breathtaking view of the vineyard my family owns, I find Honey and Dawson.

Dawson smiles at her, encouraging her to try a piece of the cake. I don't know what he said, but whatever it was, she's holding her stomach and laughing. That ring on her finger is like a shiny beacon to my current misery.

Dawson is all smiles until his gaze slips over to me. "Rya?" he says, surprised. "What are you doing here?"

I click my tongue. "Yeah, tell me about it. I could ask you the same."

Honey is quiet momentarily before saying, "So I assume you two know each other?"

"Does she know?" he asks me and then looks at Honey.

"About your best friend's dick move? Yeah, she knows. Well, sort of."

"I know enough," Honey adds, tucking a piece of her hair behind her ear.

I raise an eyebrow at her obvious nervousness around Dawson. He's hot, and I don't blame her, but I didn't expect her to act so coy. I haven't seen my sister for fourteen years, but this much is apparent—we aren't kids anymore.

"Dawson, can you give us a few minutes, please?"

He looks between us warily but leaves the room. Dawson lingers at the door and looks at me. "It's good to see you, Rya."

I give him a small smile. "You too, Dawson."

"He's apparently here to help organize things, and he's my fiancé's best man."

The way she says fiancé twists knots in my stomach. I don't even have a ring on my finger to fidget with, but I find myself wringing my hands anyway. So much time came between us as sisters, but to be reunited under these circumstances is horrible.

"Maria, can you please bring out some snacks and wine," Honey instructs a nearby servant.

"Lots of wine," I add. "Please, Maria."

She nods courteously, and I follow my sister to the garden courtyard. The view from my family home is beautiful, and a wave of relief washes over me. I'd forgotten how at ease this view put me. It's so different from the hustle and bustle of New York.

I sit across from her, and she watches me expectantly.

"Crue is a dangerous man," I tell her.

She lets out a sharp breath. "You think I don't know that? I don't really care about Crue Monti right now." I stare at her, somewhat surprised. She seemed like such a 'good girl' yesterday, like the perfect soon-to-be wife. "What I want to know is how deep this goes between the two of you. I will *not* be anyone's second pick. But you really haven't given me a choice."

"What?"

"You were the one contracted for this marriage. Not me. Do you think I don't know what type of man Crue Monti is? What he expects in a woman? Which is clearly the opposite of you."

"Ouch," I say, affronted. *Has Honey always been like this?*

"At least I'm better at hiding my reluctance."

I nod in agreement. I suppose that much hasn't changed since we were children. But what Honey wanted, she always got. Is this the first time she hasn't? Or does she want this?

"So, explain to me why I should be reconsidering my engagement to one of the most powerful and wealthiest men in all of Italy."

Maria places a tray of freshly made sandwiches on the table, vegetarian options included, and a bottle of red wine.

"No one is telling you that you have to reconsider your marriage."

She pushes out another uppity breath and pours my glass of wine before her own. "The throwing water in my fiancé's face and him losing his shit wildly over my sister tells me otherwise. Did you guys hook up?"

I take a sip of my wine and moan at its deliciousness. "On multiple occasions."

"Do you love him?" she asks.

I cough, the wine going down the wrong way.

"Do you?" I ask.

"Wow. For a bigshot American lawyer, I thought you would be better at covering things up." Honey shakes her head, picking at her sandwich. "Deflection. How dishonest of you." She stares at me expectantly. In some ways, Honey is still a little princess, but she's a woman now too. And it makes me miss her all the more.

"Because if you don't stop this, I will go through with it. I *will* be the perfect wife he asks for and uphold the Ricci name. And what will *you* do?"

I can't even look at the food while she casually eats.

"How can you so easily give away your freedom to a man you hardly know?" I ask, almost terrified of how submissive she has become.

"I'm not giving it away at all. I like my lifestyle. He's attractive. Powerful. And I no doubt will get everything I ever ask for. What is so wrong with that?"

I can't argue with her.

She continues, "As a Ricci, it is one of our roles to fulfill that duty. Contract or not. It's not like either of us can suddenly marry a nobody. No one will ever be good enough for the Ricci name. Except maybe a Monti."

I blow out a whistle. "You've been spending too much time with Papa." I laugh.

"And you've been gone for too long, sister," she replies sternly. "I've missed you all these years, and when you return, it's under these circumstances. As if

I'm being used as some pawn in Crue's game with you. Do you know how humiliated I was yesterday?"

"I didn't know he was going to come back here and propose to you," I say defensively.

"Why? Because he'd already asked you?"

My nails tap against the table as I contemplate how much I should disclose. But she deserves to know the truth. All of it. "More like Crue dragged me to the alter, and I shot him in the leg so I could run away."

Her eyes grow wide. "You shot Crue Monti and survived?"

"Everyone really gives him too much credit." I wave it off dismissively.

She leans back in her chair thoughtfully. "So now what? Are you going to take him back, or am I going through with this wedding?"

I eye Honey, her defiant chin pointed in the air. How can this be so contractual for her? Or better yet, when did I stop being the same? When did I waver when it came to Crue Monti?

Suddenly, with the responsibility in her hands, I realize I don't feel like the older sister at all. Honey so easily takes it in her stride.

I hesitate because I find I don't want to encourage the wedding but want no involvement in it either. I open my mouth and shut it again.

I don't want her marrying Crue.

But I can't have him either.

"It was only ever sex," I tell her, my voice a lot quieter than I like to acknowledge.

"If you say so. Well, the marriage is going ahead, then. And I expect you to be my maid of honor. And for you to be on your best behavior." She points a finger at me. "Now, done with the Monti contract. Tell me all about New York." It is like a switch that she flicked and has completely changed the subject on me.

A barrage of conflicting feelings hits me, and I don't know why.

But right now, I feel like I'm either going to scream or cry.

CHAPTER 64

Crue

I hate her.

The way she looks in that black dress.

The way her bronze skin and caramel locks grab my attention even through the masses of people at the Ricci home.

Numerous guests have congratulated Honey and me on our engagement. My patience grows thinner with each one who offers their well wishes. I want all of these formalities to be done because I am done with this farce.

Rya arrived thirty minutes late, and I wanted to bend her over and spank her ass for being tardy as usual. It was most likely deliberate. And it pains me to drag my gaze away from her and to my fiancée, who is the perfect hostess. I have nothing against Honey. On the contrary, she will be the perfect wife. She's pretty too.

My mother is fluttering around her and offering hand-made treats.

"You're making it too obvious," Dawson warns as he sits beside me. We're sitting in the garden's court-yard, sunset bathing the vineyard beyond and show-casing the lighter strands in Rya's hair as she speaks with her father.

I permitted Dominic the night off to be with Angel and their newborn. It also gives him a night away from my fawning mother.

"Making what obvious?" I grit through my teeth.

"Which of the Ricci sisters you really want to fuck tonight."

I glare at him.

"I tried to be the voice of reason once, and now look where we are." Dawson salutes with his glass before taking a sip.

"Your stupid fucking advice didn't work," I spit.

He laughs. "I told you to woo Rya, give her freedom."

"I don't have to woo anyone."

"That much is apparent since you're about to be a husband to the wrong sister."

My gaze drifts to Honey's finger and the oversized

rock she picked herself. It was the biggest they had. Not that I mind. The other ring I had—the one I picked for a particular princess—is still hidden away in my safe.

I watch as a man approaches Rya. His smile is suave, and his eyes are glued to her chest. My grip tightens on my glass of whisky.

I can't help myself. I'm absolutely about to pull out my gun and shoot every fucking man within Rya's vicinity.

CHAPTER 65

Rya

"Toni?" I say, surprised to see my old childhood friend. It's different to see him fully grown. I remember having a small crush on him and inviting him to my thirteenth birthday party. We had five minutes alone, and neither of us knew what to do to fill the silence.

"Well, I'll be damned," he replies with a thick accent. "I never thought I'd see the day the bigshot American lawyer returned to home soil."

"Shut up." I slap him on the shoulder. "It took me too long to come back, I know."

"It did," he says with a warm smile. His age shows slightly in the few wrinkles around his eyes. But that shy side of him is all the same. Different from a certain prick whose gaze I've felt on me all night.

"Can I get you a drink?" he offers, looking at my near-empty glass.

"That won't be necessary," Dawson cuts in, coming to my side and staring the poor guy down.

"Oh, sorry, I didn't realize you were, um..."

"No, it's not what it looks like." I point between me and Dawson.

Dawson's stare is steadfast, and it's the first time I realize how intimidating he can be.

"Are you shitting me right now?" I growl quietly.

"I could say the same to you." He leans down to whisper in my ear, "Wouldn't you rather it be me making a scene than Crue gunning down every man who's made eye contact with your tits tonight? I'm going to have to bubble-wrap you to make sure a massacre doesn't happen."

I huff out an exasperated sigh. "Crue does *not* own me. He's marrying my sister, remember."

"And how did that happen?" Dawson bites back with more fierceness than I expect from him. "I don't have any siblings, but I imagine it's not fair on Honey to be stepping into the middle of whatever chaos you two have between you."

His words hit hard.

Honey knows what she's stepping into.

But does she?

Do any of us?

I cut a brief glance in Crue's direction, and his stare is pinned on me and Dawson.

Fuck! I turn so I can't see him anymore, my heart leaping out of my chest.

"I liked you more when you spoke less and were simply pretty," I say to Dawson.

He gives me his most wicked smile. "I could say the same for you."

"Are you enjoying the party, Dawson?" Honey says in a way that breaks the tension between us. And I wonder if it's because perhaps Honey fancies him. Or is it that she simply plays hostess well? Either way, I excuse myself.

The reality is, I don't think Honey knows what she's signing up for. A man like Crue expects complete obedience, and my throat constricts at how she might falter under his gaze. She may love the lifestyle, but mostly, she has lived freely. Does she not understand the collar and chain that is Crue Monti?

I pass by Mrs. Monti, her obvious glare taking me in from head to toe, ticking up my irritation. Then again, I suppose the last time she saw me, I was supposed to marry her son and shot him instead.

CHAPTER 66

Crue

I throw back my whisky and follow her.

Because, of course, I can.

What else am I supposed to do?

Rya steps into the library and I follow her, closing the door behind us. She doesn't so much as look over her shoulder as she trails her finger along the spines of a shelf of books.

That tight black dress clings to her curves, that body my hand knows the workings of inside and out. My cock twitches at the reminder. This insufferable woman who has created so much damage in my life, and yet I find myself still drawn to her.

Obsessed.

Captivated.

Be-fucking-witched.

I can't let her go, even though everything is in motion for me to be elsewhere.

To marry someone else.

"Have you slept with her?" Rya asks her tone even.

I watch her uncomfortably, adjusting my cock.

What the fuck do I have to lose? I want to savor her if this is the last time I'll see Rya Ricci.

"You are the *only* one I think of. In those little red pieces. The way your pulse feels beneath my hand as I strangle your delicate neck."

"Stop that," Rya hisses as she finally looks over her shoulder. She walks over to the wooden desk at the end of the long room, her nails click and drag as they always do when she's thinking.

"What! Being honest? At least one of us is, princess."

She chuckles. "It must be the end of the world if Crue Monti is an example of honesty."

"When have I ever lied to you?"

"Twisting and not fully disclosing the truth is *not* being honest. That shit you pulled in New York made me do some serious questioning, especially with that fat payout I received from the Torrisi family right before their sudden demise. Care to explain that?"

I lean against the door, hitching a leg up with a

smile. "Is there much to explain, princess? I saw an opportunity and took it."

"You used me," she seethes.

"I made you rich."

"I never cared about the money," she admits quietly as she absently rifles through things on the desk. The room is dark, but there's enough light beaming in from beneath the door that I can make out her silhouette.

"Is there anything you care about?"

The question lingers in the air. Fuck going around in these circles. I stride toward her, erasing the distance between us. She's stiff at my movement as I round the desk, like she might bolt at the first chance. But I'm used to that now and have grown incredibly tired of all this bullshit. "At least one of us is willing to meet this head-on. I never considered you a coward," I say.

I reach for her face, but she slaps my hand away. I expect to see rage burning from her usually calculating gaze, but instead, I find uncontrolled tears streaming from her eyes. I freeze. Furious, unrelenting emotions boil to the surface, and I'm too stunned to know how to deal with her. Hell, she doesn't even know what to do with them.

"Stop fucking with me, Crue. You are nothing but an asshole," she says angrily as she shoves me with her finger. "You have only ever cared about yourself, so don't you dare tell me I am the coward."

I catch her finger and pull her to me, making sure my other hand rests over my gun. I won't fall for that a second time. She looks up at me with wet lashes. The smell of her perfume and her body's comfort against mine consume me.

She feels right.

She is *mine*.

A tap on the door sounds before Mr. Ricci enters.

Rya steps away from me, rubbing at her eyes. Her father looks between us before he calls out to Rya, who obediently follows. I want to grab her, pull her back to me but something stops me. And it might be the glare Mr. Ricci throws me or the weight of how fucked-up this all is.

It was meant to be simple.

Get married.

Sign the contract.

And it would all be mine.

Yet, since returning from New York, the edge of my hunger has wavered. And I know exactly why. It's all tied to this little vixen who shuts the door behind her.

And once again she is running from me.

I stare out over the lake.

I'd taken Papa's most prized Ferrari to my favorite of our many family homes. It's a nice change of scenery, driving the car through the rolling hills and ending up here. I rest the glass of wine casually on my knee.

When I think back on it, I always liked this house more because it was smaller than the others. We occasionally entertained a few guests here, but this place was meant for the family.

Last night had been a disaster.

Between Honey and Crue, I decided I couldn't participate in the wedding. They will be having their second engagement party at the Monti house right now, and I sure as hell wasn't going. In fact, I have purchased an airline ticket back home for tomorrow. Sure, I'd only been here for less than a week, but I wasn't *me* here.

Crying in front of Crue Monti, no less, was a new low for me. I haven't cried since... well, ever. But this man opens me up more than he has the right to. He's under my skin now as much as I am a part of him.

I'm determined to deny him and this thing between us. But that sudden realization last night when he touched me, the sadness to know he wasn't mine anymore—if he ever was—was devastating. For so long, I had pushed him away behind excuses.

He's a criminal.

He's a killer.

He's possessive, short-tempered, and all asshole.

But I've come to love every single one of those things about him. And that makes me devastatingly aware of the power Crue holds over me. And so I do what I know when a powerful man has control over my life. I flee.

A loud noise comes from behind me. I should be alone out here, so I turn around to see what it was. I step around the house and down the few stairs as I watch, dazed, at Crue's black sports car pulling up. He gets out, dressed neatly in a black suit.

How did he find me?

I grip my wine glass tightly as he beelines straight for me. When he reaches me, I finally release the breath I was holding. We stand in front of one another, neither of us speaking, just staring at each other.

I love him.

That thought rocks my soul, cracks it wide open, and worse than that it hurts.

I love him.

Fuck, I also hate him.

I can't love the man my sister is about to marry. I simply can't. We will not be those people. I will not allow it.

I go to open my mouth, but he steps forward, halting my words.

"We called it off," he rushes to say.

I'm shocked. Crue told me he had to get married.

We called it off.

"Why?" I ask.

We're so close now, I can smell him. Everywhere. He is taking over my senses, and he's all I can imagine and all that I want.

"Because it's you I want. Let's lie to each other all you want."

"That sounds lethal."

"Give me your lethal vows, princess."

So much raw emotion bubbles to the surface, but all I can say is, "What about Honey?"

"She sent me here."

Before I can tell him I love him, he pulls me to him, and his mouth covers mine. His kiss steals my breath, and I drop the wine glass. I hear it smash on the ground beside me, but I don't care. My arms wrap around his shoulders, and his hands cup my ass, and he lifts me, my legs circling his waist.

"I love you, Miss Ricci," he says between heavy breaths.

A tear leaves my eye, and he pulls back, his tongue darting out to lick it away before I look up at him with wet lashes. "I think I love you too," I tell him.

"*Think?*" he growls, and I watch anger radiate from him. He bites his lip, then smashes his mouth back to mine. Crue takes a few steps away from the glass, and before I know it, my back hits the dirt, and he's hovering over me. "You *think*?" he says, standing. Then he's tearing off his shirt in one swift movement and unbuckling his belt.

He glares down at me as he orders, "Pull up the dress."

I do as he says.

His pants hang open, and I can see his cock straining against his briefs. "Now, turn over." I look at him, confused. "On your stomach, princess. *Now*." I try not to put my face in the dirt, but it's hard. When I look back at him, I see him smirking, his belt still in his hand. "You wore red."

"Yes."

"Did you hope to show me?"

"No," I reply. And that's when Crue moves, his hand touching me between my legs. The lace there is already wet, and he looks me in the eyes as I stare back at him.

"Lie." And he snaps the belt on my ass.

I scream, but it's not from pain. It's from the surprise. *Why the fuck do I like it?*

"I have dreamed of making this ass red." He rubs his hand over my heated skin, again dipping between my legs. I move them further apart to give him better access, but he pulls his hand away. When I glance back at him, I see him dip his fingers into his mouth before he puts them back between my legs. "So fucking wet already." He tugs at my G-string, removing it easily, then quickly slides two fingers inside me. He groans and asks, "Did you wear them for me?"

Ignoring his question, I say, "That was expensive."

"Get on your knees." I do as he says. "Tell me the truth, and I will reward you."

I turn my face away and feel him move, but I don't

look back. Part of me is hoping he'll spank me again, while the other wants him to fuck me already.

"Yes, I wore them for you," I whisper.

His hands slide between my legs, and he pulls me back, my fingers scraping in the dirt. My knees are now on either side of his head, and he pulls me down, his face directly under my pussy as he starts to move his mouth.

Holy shit.

Holy mother of fuck.

He fucks me with his tongue, and I ride his face as if it's my favorite attraction.

It is.

It totally fucking is.

Before I can stop myself, I push myself up to just my knees. And when I look down, Crue's face is still there between my legs, his hands on my ass, controlling every movement as he fucks me with his mouth. His gaze is locked on me. It's hot, primal, and I'm unsure what to do as my body shakes. He slaps my ass, and I come hard. His mouth slows down, and before I can collapse, he moves me with ease down his body so I'm over his cock. He slides in easily and begins to thrust. My hands spear through his hair, and I grip it before I find his mouth and kiss him.

I taste myself all over him, but I don't care.

His cock is moving slowly, then fast, then slowly again. It's like a rhythm I didn't know I needed. That is until he slows and thrusts in and out of me with such gentle torture that I rip my mouth away from his and slam down on his cock.

He tears the dress from my body, leaving me completely naked. My hands find my breasts, and I squeeze them as I pick up the rhythm and start riding him back and forth with a pace so good that it doesn't take long before I'm coming again. He grips my ass, picking up speed where I start to lack, and lifts from the ground, his mouth finding my nipple, his teeth biting down.

And I come.

And I come.

And I come.

Fuck.

I lean forward, biting his shoulder as he presses kisses to my neck.

"See how perfect you are for me?" he asks, still thrusting. "How much your body craves mine?" He bites me. "So delicious, princess, the way your sweet pussy milks me. I'm number one, aren't I?"

"Yes!" I breathe the word out.

Just as he comes, I collapse on him, and he chuckles and lies back down, still inside of me.

"I was always number one, wasn't I?"

I laugh. "Not sure I should tell you that," I reply.

He flips me quickly, and I yelp as he leaves my body but covers it straight away.

"Do you want to be spanked again?"

"No." I smile. "Maybe." Crue reaches for something, and I freeze when I see the familiar ring box. He lays it next to us. Both of us looking at it silently for a moment.

"Marry me," he says.

My heart is pulsing, but I can't deny this man anymore.

I can't let anyone else have him.

It's selfish.

It's consuming.

And he's mine.

I lean up and kiss him. "Only on my terms."

He chuckles, and before I know it, he's back inside of me, and I glance at the ring. It's delicate with a pink sparkle. It's not huge, which I'd hate, but it's a commitment—one I've been running away from my entire life.

CHAPTER 68
Crue

After our explosive reunion, I carried her to bed. Rya was tired and asleep before her head hit the pillow. But before I took my place beside her, I slipped the engagement ring on her finger. She starts to shift, but before she has the chance to escape the bed, I pull her back with my arm around her stomach. Then I rub my notably hard cock against her ass.

She chuckles. "Calm down. I'm just going to make us coffee."

"You seem to make a habit out of running, princess."

She twists in my arms and levels me with a stare. "And one thing I can depend on you for is your next-level stalker skills."

"Oh, but Miss Ricci, I have so many other skills to offer."

She smiles and presses a possessive claim to my lips, her hips rolling against my cock.

"We need to sort out our contract before I let you get away with any more of this."

My eyes spring open. "Contract? You really know how to kill a mood, don't you."

"I am a lawyer, after all," she teases as she pushes away. "At least I offer mercy by making you a coffee first." That's when she stills, her gaze falling to her hand. Then, those eyes I love so much raise to stare back at me.

"Why do I have the ring on?" she asks.

"Because it's yours."

"We haven't agreed on anything."

"I'll agree to whatever you want. I want *you*," I say simply,

She glances back at her hand and then walks out, not saying another word or taking her eyes off the ring.

WHEN SHE DOESN'T RETURN, I pull on my pants and step down the staircase. Rya is sitting on the couch, all business-like, in my shirt. Her bronze skin is on display as she crosses her legs deliberately, making sure to give me a good look at that sweet cunt of hers.

"If you could please take a seat, Mr. Monti." She suggests the chair across from her.

I pick up the coffee she made and watch her appreciatively.

The morning sun and water behind her produce a halo of sorts around the woman I would consider anything but saintly.

"I've drafted up a new contract," she states.

"A new contract?" I raise a curious brow as I take a sip of the coffee. It's ironic since that's what got us into this mess in the first place.

"You're forced to take a wife within two weeks, correct?"

"Correct," I grit out, unsure as to where she's going with this. I have always made that abundantly clear.

"And you can't possibly get out of it?"

"Not unless I kill over twenty founding fathers, which I am not entirely opposed to."

Her gaze darts to me, and I see the quick calculation there.

She throws her hair over her shoulder and says, "Then they'll get a wedding. We *will* marry. I *will* take your name. But so help me God, if you piss me off, I *will* become unfaithful and fuck you off at the first chance I get and continue to do so until you are driven insane."

The noise that comes from my throat is not entirely human. "I'm done with this cat-and-mouse game, princess."

"Then don't be a possessive asshole."

"But you like that part of me," I say with a narrowed gaze.

She hides her smile, all lawyer-like. "I'm not done. I don't know if I want kids. But the families don't have to know that. This contract states that should I choose not to give you any heirs, I am not obligated to do so."

"I need an heir, Rya."

"Do you want me or an heir?" Her nail lightly begins to tap on the contract as she considers me. I'm sure as hell not going to give her any reason to run again. But, surely, she knows me well enough to know I'll get what I want in the end.

"I've always wanted you," I tell her. "I will always choose you."

Her breath hitches and she looks back at the contract. "And if that happens and I do not produce an heir, then I find myself slightly biased toward the next-in-line heir, Alessia. Who so happens to also be our godchild."

I hold my tongue. She *will* be giving me an heir.

"No bugging my phone," she continues.

"Scratch that out."

She looks at me with an edge to her gaze and then takes a sharp intake of breath as if deciding something. "Fine. I will remain in New York."

"You will move into my penthouse."

"I will consider it. But I won't sell my apartment, so I can retreat there when you become too overbearing. And you are *not* allowed to break in."

"It's not breaking in if I'm your husband," I grumble.

"Crue." She places the paper on her lap and gives me an expression that is so unimpressed I want to fuck her demanding, filthy mouth until she cries.

She seems to be enjoying these negotiations. "Is that all, princess? If so, come and sit on my cock like a good girl."

A devilish smile spreads across her face as she sets down her coffee and steps around the table. She straddles my hips as one of my fingers slips into her sweet pussy that's already wet and waiting for me.

She pushes the paper and pen to my chest.

"Well, Mr. Monti, do we have a deal?" she asks as she casually undoes my belt, her soft fingers gripping around my hard, throbbing cock. She leans over and whispers into my ear, her natural fragrance flaring my nostrils, "Sign this, and I'll wear that anklet of yours every day so everyone knows who I belong to."

I continue to roll my thumb over her sweet pussy as she glides her hand up and down my cock.

"They *will* know who you belong to in name alone," I growl, then I nod to her ring. "And because of that."

She chuckles and taps on the contract I'm still holding. "Only you can make that happen. Sign, asshole," she says in a sweet and sickly tone.

CHAPTER 69

Rya

Dear Miss Ricci

Should you have cold feet in advance of today's event, know that I will literally hunt you down to the ends of the earth, and you will be severely punished.

Reply.

Crue

Dear Mr. Monti

I was told my husband would be a sweet type of fellow. So how did I end up with someone so crude, brash, and *still probably only in my top two at best?*

That is the only time I will reply.

Your Betrothed

I fight the burning heat that feels like it's clawing up my chest. I think about the new contract Crue and I signed. And now I have to uphold my end of the bargain. But shit, if that didn't make it awkward with the hundreds of people sitting in chairs and staring at us now.

And instead of the Ricci daughter he announced at the engagement party, Honey stands as the maid of honor. But by the way she's clearly eye fucking Dawson across the room, I think she's grateful I took this place.

The exact thing I ran away from all of those years is where I have ended up now.

Beside one of the most dangerous men in the world.

Possessive.

Controlling.

A complete asshole.

Crue is every one of these things and so much more.

But despite that, I sure as hell won't let him walk all over me.

What am I considered now? A criminal defense lawyer with the intention to open her own firm when I returned to New York. And... a boss?

When I asked Crue what his men would call me from now on, he laughed before pulling me back into his lap at the lake house. His hand had brushed against my cheek, wiping away a few strands of loose hair. "You will be revered as my queen. And anyone who tries to speak to you casually or indirectly without my permission will end up dead."

I smile now at that memory, looking into the dark, molten eyes of Crue that most certainly promise all the wicked thrills to come. And if he pisses me off, I'll knee him in the balls or possibly shoot him in the other leg. After all, it's a wife's duty to keep her husband in line, isn't it?

Running my hands down my dress, I walk to the end, where my husband waits.

He leans in and whispers for only me to hear,

"Ready to give me your lethal vows, wife."

And I can't help but smirk as that word leaves his mouth.

Who knew it would create butterflies in my stomach.

Who knew I'd love this man with everything I am?

He did.

That's who.

Asshole.

Also by T.L. Smith

Black (Black #1)

Red (Black #2)

White (Black #3)

Green (Black #4)

Kandiland

Pure Punishment (Standalone)

Antagonize Me (Standalone)

Degrade (Flawed #1)

Twisted (Flawed #2)

Distrust (Smirnov Bratva #1) FREE

Disbelief (Smirnov Bratva #2)

Defiance (Smirnov Bratva #3)

Dismissed (Smirnov Bratva #4)

Lovesick (Standalone)

Lotus (Standalone)

Savage Collision (A Savage Love Duet book 1)

Savage Reckoning (A Savage Love Duet book 2)

Buried in Lies

Distorted Love (Dark Intentions Duet 1)

Sinister Love (Dark Intentions Duet 2)

Cavalier (Crimson Elite #1)

Anguished (Crimson Elite #2)

Conceited (Crimson Elite #3)

Insolent (Crimson Elite #4)

Playette

Love Drunk

Hate Sober

Heartbreak Me (Duet #1)

Heartbreak You (Duet #2)

My Beautiful Poison

My Wicked Heart

My Cruel Lover

Chained Hands

Locked Hearts

Sinful Hands

Shackled Hearts

Reckless Hands

Arranged Hearts

Unlikely Queen

A Villain's Kiss

A Villain's Lies

Moments of Malevolence

Moments of Madness

Connect with T.L Smith by tlsmithauthor.com

Also by Kia Carrington Russell

Mine for the Night, New York Nights Book 1

Us for the Night, New York Nights Book 2

Stranded for the Night, New York Nights Book 3

Token Huntress, Token Huntress Book 1

Token Vampire, Token Huntress Book 2

Token Wolf, Token Huntress Book 3

Token Phantom, Token Huntress Book 4

Token Darkness, Token Huntress Book 5

Token Kingdom, Token Huntress Book 6

The Shadow Minds Journal

T.L. Smith

USA Today Best Selling Author T.L. Smith loves to write her characters with flaws so beautiful and dark you can't turn away. Her books have been translated into several languages. If you don't catch up with her in her home state of Queensland, Australia you can usually find her travelling the world, either sitting on a beach in Bali or exploring Alcatraz in San Francisco or walking the streets of New York.

Connect with me tlsmithauthor.com

Kia Carrington-Russell

Australian Author, Kia Carrington-Russell is known for her recognizable style of kick a$$ heroines, fast-paced action, enemies to lovers and romance that dances from light to dark in multiple genres including Fantasy, Dark and Contemporary Romance.

Obsessed with all things coffee, food and travel, Kia is always seeking out her next adventure internationally. Now back in her home country of Australia, she takes her Cavoodle, Sia along morning walks on beautiful coastline beaches, building worlds in the sea breezes and contemplating which deliciously haunting story to write next.

Made in the USA
Middletown, DE
16 July 2024